B. J.

Atwell

2012 A.D.:
The Pavelic Legacy

(Book 1 of 3 of "The Genesis Coverup"

Trilogy)

Emerald Publishing Group

New York

Emerald Publishing Group
65 Fifth Street
Glens Falls, NY 12801.

ISBN 978-0-6151-4492-4

10 9 8 7 6 5 4 3 2 1

Printed In the United States of America

For Gail and Lucy
for your unwavering support

And it came to pass, as they went on, and talked, that, behold, there appeared a chariot of fire, and horses of fire, and parted them both asunder, and Elijah went up by a whirlwind into heaven.

And Elisha saw it, and he cried My father, my father, the chariot of Israel, and the horsemen thereof, And he saw him no more; and he took hold of his own clothes, and rent them in two pieces.

Kings 2:11-12

FOREWORD

People often ask fiction writers where their ideas or inspiration comes from: I have had a lifelong interest in both biblical literature and World War II and most fiction plots can be answered by the question, 'what if?'

Adolf Hitler was obsessed with finding religious objects of faith, especially The Ark of the Covenant. What if he found it and what if it changed orthodox church teachings significantly?

The story you are about to read answers both of those 'what if' questions.

SPECIAL NOTE

To my international friends: many American word processing systems have some annoying limitations; please be aware of the following:

The word, *Fuhrer*, is lacking the proper 'umlat.'

The word, *naivete*, is lacking the 'accent acute'.

Please accept my apology for this shortcoming.

B. J. Atwell

PROLOGUE

Lake George, New York
June 12, 2005

The first bullet struck Penny's grandfather in the right shoulder as he stood from cleaning the fireplace. He fell to his knees as she rushed to him. Another bullet hit the stonework on the right side of the fireplace and Penny saw her grandmother move in her peripheral vision. She had been struck in the right side of the head by a chunk of the stonework shattered by the bullet. She appeared to have passed out in her favorite chair next to the fireplace. There were two more shots that went harmlessly into the wall above the fireplace mantel, then it was quiet. Penny ran to the kitchen and brought back two towels she had soaked in cold water. Although her mind was spinning, trying to imagine what the hell was happening, she had her grandfather holding a compress to his shoulder and wrapped the other towel around her *Grandmere's* head. She ran for the telephone and called 911. She could see that her *Grandpere* was going into shock, his shoulder must be shattered, and the towel had turned a bright crimson in seconds. She prayed the ambulance would not be long in coming. She grabbed pillows from the sofa and elevated both his and her *Grandmere's*

legs and heard the faint klaxon of the ambulance in the distance as she put pressure on his horrible wound.

The emergency medical team did not waste a second, or motion, in assessing the situation and before she knew it they were en route to the Glens Falls Hospital, the closest facility to Lake George, with the police in tow. Penny's mind would not be still. Who could possibly want to harm her grandparents? How could such violence invade this small lake resort community at the foot of her beloved Adirondack Mountains? She had spent every summer, since the age of ten, exploring the lake and the mountains. When Penny's parents had been killed in an automobile accident when she was ten, she went to live with her grandparents in their condominium in New York City. Her grandfather taught Romance Languages at Columbia and he and *Grandmere* spent their summers at Lake George. They had built a large chalet at Bolton Landing and she and her grandparents explored every inch of the lake by boat and hiked deep into the heart of the mountains until her grandparents began to lose their stamina, their youth.

It took nearly two hours before the emergency room doctor was able to tell Penny how serious the injuries were after ordering extensive radiological studies of both grandparents. "Ms Brooks, both your grandparents injuries are serious; made more serious because of their ages. Your grandfather's shoulder is going to require extensive

surgery; there are many bone and bullet fragments to be removed. I have called-in an orthopedic surgeon, one of the best in the business, because there will have to be considerable reconstruction of the shoulder joint, but none of this can commence until he is more stable. He lost a lot of blood and was in shock when he arrived. It could have been a lot worse without the care both you and the EMT's gave him. It's going to be rocky for the next 48 hours, but I rate his chances of recovery as fair. Your grandmother is still unconscious. She has a serious concussion from the stone fragment lodged in the side of her head. When the stone struck her, it caused the brain to bounce against the opposite side of the cranium. We see the typical swelling from this kind of injury, but no bleeding into the brain, the bleeding is epidural and not sub-dural. The stone removal is not a difficult procedure, but it could be awhile before the swelling is controlled and she regains consciousness. Both will be admitted to the surgical wing of the hospital and I fear you have some tense hours ahead, young lady. The police insist on talking to you as soon as possible; they need your statement and your grandfather's shock has been reversed and despite the pain medication we gave him, he insists on talking to you. I suggest you see him first; we need to keep him calm." Tears were streaming down her face as she opened the curtain that surrounded her grandfather's bed. He looked deathly pale, but the gray tinge that so

frightened her when they left the chalet was gone. She was a little angry that the nurses pushed her away when they first arrived, but she knew there was little room for her with all the people administering to both her grandparents. His eyes seemed to light up as she neared his bed. "Oh Penny, I am so glad they let you in! I need you to make a telephone call for me. Please call Anthony West and tell him what happened. The number is 202-555-5555. It is a direct line."

"Anthony West? You mean the former CIA Director? What does he have to do with what has happened? With you?"

"Just do as I ask, Luv! (He still hadn't lost his British accent or expressions!) I'll explain as soon as we have a little more privacy. But, please, do it from a pay phone as soon as possible and for god's sake don't mention it to anyone! *I mean anyone*; especially not the police! Tell him I need to talk to him, his earliest. Write it down; again, the number is 202-555-5555. What have they told you about your grandmother?" She told him what the doctor said and he pushed her out of the room. "Now, go tell the police what happened and make that call." If he could issue orders like that, Penny was convinced that he was going to make a speedy recovery. She peeked in another curtain and there was a nurse with her grandmother, who was, of course, still unconscious. Penny decided it was time to face the police. It went fairly quickly because she couldn't tell them much. There were

four shots from a high powered rifle (She knew guns, *Grandpere* was an expert marksman and taught her to shoot when she was 16). She couldn't describe anyone; only where she thought the shots were coming from. When they were finished, she headed for the hospital lobby, where she knew there was a pay phone, to call Anthony West.

He picked up the phone on the second ring, "Mr. West, my name is Penelope Penrose-Brooks, my grandfather is Laurence Penrose-Brooks. There has been a terrible shooting and both of my grandparents have been seriously injured. My grandfather insisted I call you as soon as possible. He wants to talk to you, at your earliest convenience."

"Good Lord! How serious are their injuries?" came the immediate reply. Penny described what the doctor had told her. "Tell your grandfather that I will fly up as soon as I can arrange a flight." Penny was more than a little surprised at this news. She knew her grandfather knew a lot of people, but a former director of the CIA? What was *Grandpere's* connection to this man? To the government? He was a professor! She knew he was a soldier during World War II, fighting for England, and he met her grandmother in occupied France, but that was a long time ago. Could the shooting have anything to do with events that old?

Penny's grandfather's surgery was the following morning and

the surgeon believed that he would regain full motion after rehabilitation therapy. There had been no change in *Grandmere's* condition. Mr. West arrived just as her grandfather was returning to his room from the recovery room. They greeted each other as old friends and then her grandfather started with the orders, again. "Penny, I need to speak to Mr. West, alone. Would you go to the head guy, here, if you have to, and arrange for your grandmother to be transferred to this room? I want to keep an eye on her." Penny went to the nurse's station and began the transfer request.

Penny was still at the nurse's station when Mr. West came up beside her and spoke, "I don't want to frighten you, Ms. Brooks, but I am going to arrange for someone to stand guard outside your grandparents' room until we find out what this is all about." She nodded her head, and had the distinct feeling that Mr. West knew what this was all about. She was determined to get the truth from her grandfather. "I have to leave the building for a few hours, perhaps we could meet for dinner?" he continued. "I will be staying at the Queensbury Hotel and I understand the food is pretty good. Could you join me at 6 o'clock?" She agreed and returned to her grandfather. He had fallen asleep, so she wasn't going to get the truth from him for awhile. It was about an hour later that they wheeled her grandmother into the room after removing the empty bed from the other side of the room. She had a large bandage around her head and appeared to be in a deep sleep. The nurses fussed over her for about a half-hour and then the room was quiet. Penny sat holding her hand for awhile and then she began to grow sleepy, herself. She awoke with a start two hours later; both grandparents were sleeping and she had only a half-hour to freshen-up as best she could to meet Mr. West for dinner. There was a guard sitting outside the door when she left. It did provide a measure of comfort to see him and to see that he was armed.

The Queensbury Hotel is in the heart of Glens Falls, a sprawling small city that is the half-way mark for tourists visiting from Canada on their way New York City and vice versa. It is only nine miles from Lake George. The lake's resident population is small, but swells to over fifty to one-hundred thousand during the height of the summer season. Glens Falls also plays host to many of these visitors. Penny is an avid walker so made her way to the hotel on foot. As an investigative reporter for the Wall Street Journal, she walked hundreds of miles a year, pounding the sidewalks of New York City and cities around the world. Penny was, currently, on a leave of absence from the newspaper, helping her grandparents to move to Lake George permanently. At 30, with her own by-line at the newspaper and one who travels constantly, she was still enjoying being single, unencumbered by the responsibilities of a husband and children.

Penny had another two weeks of leave and her grandparents are really going to need her. She was thinking of returning to work early because her grandparents were all settled, but that had all changed. She spotted Anthony West sitting at an outside table of the Garden-On-The-Park, a popular feature of the Queensbury and made her way to his table. He was drinking something in a tall glass that looked appropriate for the unusually hot weather for early June. As she sat he spoke, "I'm having a Tom Collins that is quite good." The waitress came from taking an order from a table three tables away and Penny ordered the same. "How were your grandparents when you left the hospital, Ms Brooks? Any change to report?" He had a look of deep concern on his face and Penny wondered how close he was to her grandparents. She could not remember ever meeting him during the 8 years she lived in the same apartment with her grandparents. She left for college at the age of eighteen and only visited for brief periods during summer breaks and, of course, holidays. Even as a student she had the same travel bug that her father had. During most summers she was spending the allowance provided by a trust fund that her father established on the day that she was born. He was a very successful author of books involving the government and foreign affairs. He was often one of the "talking heads" on cable news shows that needed an expert. He and her mother were driving from their home on Long

Island to one of those interminable dinners where one 'had' to make an appearance when they were killed by a truck driver who had fallen asleep at the wheel. He survived. Penny's parents were killed instantly. The driver was only charged with a minor infraction!

"They were asleep when I left the hospital and have been so all afternoon. Mr. West, how do you know my grandparents? How did you meet?" She knew that Mr. West was much younger than her grandfather's 88 years. He was probably her father's age which would make him around sixty years old. They seemed unlikely cohorts.

"My father and your grandfather were in World War II together. They remained good friends until my father's death just a year ago. I know much of their history together," he replied. She was more than a little discomfited that he seemed to know more about her own grandfather than she did.

"Mr. West, do you have any idea what this shooting is about, or do you think it was just a random thing? Some nut showing his prowess with a rifle; and in broad daylight!" He seemed to give it a lot of thought before he replied.

"Your grandfather said I would not be able to keep the truth from you and I should tell you the whole story, but we cannot do it here, Ms Brooks. Let's have a nice, quiet dinner and then we can go to my room and speak in private." They both ordered the grilled salmon and ate with very little discussion. When they reached his room on the mezzanine, she was delighted to see that he had a sitting room and she wouldn't be sitting on his bed listening to him tell her grandfather's story. He also had a bar set-up on a small table and they each held a scotch and soda as they chose their respective seats.

He began without a lot of preamble, "Your grandmother saw someone a couple of days ago who is supposed to be long dead. She went to the Lake George Arts Festival as she does almost every year and saw a man known as the *Sadist of Croatia,* who was closely associated with the *Ustashe* - the fascist regime established in Yugoslavia during the war. He is an old man, now, but she recognized him by his cold, steel-blue eyes and she has good reason to remember him; she had an horrific encounter with him." He paused, presumably to see if Penny had digested this news.

"Even so," she began, "why would this old man want to kill my grandparents after sixty years? Isn't all that business over and pretty much forgotten?" Or, at least, that was what she wanted to believe.

"There seems to be little doubt that he is behind the attack on your grandparents, but the *why* must be more than the revelation that he is still alive, or he would not have exposed himself with this violence. He could have simply disappeared, again. Of course, he could be returned to Germany for war crimes, if captured, but both your

grandfather and I believe that there is more to this business. The local police are searching the motels that service the Lake George region to see if they can find him, but I do not hold out much hope. I think your grandparents must know something that, perhaps, they do not know they know. I think your grandfather, as soon as he is able, is going to have to relive those old memories to see if we can discover what is behind this attack. After the war, your grandfather remained in France working as a translator with those reclaiming and returning some of the art treasures looted during the war. Perhaps there is something he encountered during this period that can explain this apparent on-going threat to the surviving Nazis."

Penny was told she could not return to the chalet because it was still a crime scene, so she decided to stay at the Queensbury Hotel for the night. She went back to the hospital to see if there was any change in either grandparent's condition. Her grandfather had finally surrendered to all the pain medication. She was told he had been awake for a little while, but only long enough to receive more medication. He was asleep and there was no change in her grandmother's condition. She returned to the hotel for the night.

Penny's grandfather was quite alert the following morning. She didn't arrive at the hospital until nearly noon and Anthony West was sitting in a chair next to her grandfather's bed. She pulled another

chair to the other side of his bed after checking on *Grandmere*.

"You are just in time, Penny," spoke her grandfather. "Tony has asked me to relive some very unpleasant memories to see if we can discover why the *Sadist of Croatia* wants your grandmother and me dead, after all these years." She made herself comfortable as *Grandpere* began to tell his story.

Chapter One

Twenty-four hours after issuing an ultimatum to Germany to withdraw from Poland, on September 3, 1939, the United Kingdom and France declared war on Germany. The United Kingdom's army began to immediately dispatch the British Expeditionary Force to help defend France; by 1940, there were fourteen divisions under BEF command. The Royal Air Force also sent significant forces to France at the start of hostilities.

On May 10, 1940, Germany invaded the Benelux and German troops entered France through the Ardennes on May 13. Allied forces were expecting a re-run of the World War I Schlieffen Plan and were in Flanders and were cutoff from the French heartland. As a result, the Battle of France was shorter than pre-war thought conceived, with France surrendering after only six weeks; the United Kingdom was left to stand alone. During the Battle of France, the British prime minister, Neville Chamberlain resigned, to be replaced by Winston Churchill, who had opposed negotiation with Hitler. Fortunately for the United

Kingdom, much of its army escaped capture from the northern French port of Dunkirk. Three-hundred thirty-thousand troops were pulled off the beaches (two-hundred thirty-thousand were British), but almost all of the army's heavy equipment had to be abandoned in France, many of the soldiers even had to abandon their rifles.

In the Battle of Britain, the German failure to achieve air superiority marked a major turning point in the war. Hitler, having grown impatient with the failure to destroy the RAF, ordered a change in strategy from the battle for the skies to the bombing of major British cities; the Blitz was intended to destroy morale and industry. In May of 1941, it became clear to the German high command that the *Luftwaffe* was not likely to gain superiority over Britain anytime soon; significant German forces in France were reassigned to the expanding German eastern front. In retrospect, this is where Hitler made his first fatal mistake.

Winston Churchill and Hugh Dalton initiated the SOE: Special Operations Executive (often called the "Baker Street Irregulars" after Sherlock Holmes' fictional group of spies) in July of 1940. It was to be a mechanism for conducting warfare by means other than direct military engagement. Designated as 'Section D' of MI6, its mission was to encourage and facilitate espionage and sabotage behind enemy lines; to serve as a focal point for the formation and coordination of

resistance movements.

Laurence Penrose-Brooks was recruited to Section "F" (for France) in the Summer of 1940; he had just received his doctorate in Romance languages from Oxford and had already been offered a teaching position at Oxford, but wanted to play some part in the war effort. He was commissioned a Lieutenant and began training at Wanborough Manor, Guildford, to parachute into occupied France and serve as a liaison officer between the resistance groups in the alpine region and the SOE. He followed Georges Begue, who was the first to drop into France, in May of 1941, to set up radio communications.

Penrose-Brooks was to establish himself at *Lac d'Annency*, where he would be posing as the cousin of a family already actively involved in a significant resistance movement. His facility with the language and familiarity with the region made him the ideal agent for this region of France. During his years at University, he spent many of his holidays skiing at *Grenoble* and summers at his family's chalet on beautiful *Lac d'Annency*. While only twenty-four years old, he demonstrated a maturity and sense of duty that pleased his training officer.

As the parachute opened, Laurence could still feel the rumble of the plane's vibration in his legs; he hoped it would not affect his landing; he could not afford a broken leg at the outset of his duties. As he rolled upon landing, he could see lights approaching and was relieved to recognize the face in a photograph that he had studied - Guy Descartes, the resistance leader of a small group operating out of the lake region. There was a group of six people with him; one a young woman he knew to be Guy's sister, Giselle, a famous skier. Their cousin, Jean, had been killed only a few months ago. Laurence looked enough like him in build and coloring to get by posing as this cousin. No one, except family, knew he had been killed in the premature detonation of unstable explosives to be used to blow up a German supply train. There wasn't enough of him left to bury.

Three of the men with Guy were retrieving the supplies that had been dropped with him while Laurence shook hands with the Descartes. "It is good to finally meet you both; I have heard much about your activities in the region and I am looking forward to working with you. I carry with me a fake bill of sale that gives Jean Descartes ownership of my family's chalet where I will establish my headquarters. Shall we go there, first?" asked Laurence.

"If you wish," replied Guy, "it has been quiet in the region, tonight, but we can expect to encounter Germans who have heard your plane. We must move quickly - you are now Jean Descartes? *Oui?*

"*Oui*," replied Laurence, "we are now cousins!" They moved

quickly into the thin woods near the drop zone and were fortunate to trek to the chalet without any German interference. Within the hour they were all sitting around the dining room table drinking coffee that had been in the cupboard, unopened, since the Penrose-Brooks' last visit to the chalet in the summer of 1938. It still tasted better than what passed for coffee in England these days. Despite his British heritage, Laurence had always preferred coffee over tea. He wanted the boost of energy the caffeine provided.

They spent two hours going over German troop strength, the location of Gestapo headquarters, the operations planned by the group and their connections to other resistance movements in the area. Laurence disbursed some of the supplies that had arrived with him: handguns, rifles and ammunition. They were awed to learn about Laurence's new gun, created by the SOE, that made no sound. Laurence's *welrod* became a trusted ally as did his *welbike,* a light weight bicycle that folded and could be carried on his back when the bike could not be used. It was nearly dawn before Laurence finally fell asleep in his own room in his own family's chalet in occupied France.

The next few months were a frenzy of activity, racing from one project to another, one resistance group to another in an attempt to combine these resistance groups into a strong cohesive force against the Germans. They were beginning to make a large impact on German supply lines, so much so that it came to Hitler's attention. The Gestapo forces were enhanced in *Grenoble* to track down these groups and destroy them. Anyone found helping these groups was shot on sight. For every German soldier killed, ten French people were lined up and shot to atone - men, women and children. Just as difficult as skirting the Gestapo was identifying those Frenchmen collaborating with the Vichy government. Laurence lived with the fear that it would be a Frenchman who might know his family spent summers in the area and would recognize him and turn him over to the Gestapo. He was prepared to kill himself, if this happened, and that possibility became more painful when he was forced to recognize that he had fallen hopelessly in love with Giselle Descartes. She played a larger role in the resistance under Laurence's tutelage. She had been France's Olympic hopeful in downhill skiing in 1940, but of course, those games were not held. She was taught to use her expertise to serve as a courier to the many resistance groups in the alpine region around *Grenoble* and *Lac d'Annency*.

In September 1942, Guy Descartes was captured and killed when he did not relent under merciless Gestapo torture. Giselle was devastated at the loss of her brother, her only close relative, but vowed to carry on with her duties. A few months after his loss, Giselle and Laurence were secretly married by the equivalent of a justice of the peace who worked in one of the resistance groups and she moved into the chalet. Laurence reported this situation to SOE headquarters; they were not overjoyed, but were so happy with his performance that they looked the other way. Everyone understood the intensity of life in occupied France and could not begrudge their soldiers whatever moments of happiness they could find. In late October of 1942, the SOE informed Laurence that they had intercepted a communication indicating the *Sadist of Croatia,* an *Oberstleutnant* Karl Krueger, was on his way to *Grenoble* to recover from a serious gunshot wound to the stomach. Laurence's orders were to assassinate him, if at all possible. It was nearly two months before Krueger was finally spotted at a restaurant in *Grenoble*. He was living in a large chalet at the foot of *Mount Blanc*. A team was assigned to keep track of his movements while a plan was hatched to assassinate him, but before this plan could be executed Giselle was captured by the Gestapo. She was being tortured at Gestapo headquarters in *Grenoble* and it was learned that Krueger was in charge of her interrogation. On Christmas Eve of 1942, a large contingent of combined resistance groups executed a plan to free Giselle and blow-up Gestapo headquarters in *Grenoble;* they succeeded.

Laurence went nearly mad when he saw Giselle's condition - she was near death. Both of her legs had been crushed - battered repeatedly with some heavy object. She was unconscious - probably in shock and her breathing was slow and labored. A local doctor, working with the resistance, did what he could, but she had to get to a hospital. After arguing most of the night with SOE headquarters in England, a plane was dispatched to pick up Giselle and fly her to England. On Christmas Day, 1942, Giselle and Laurence were separated until France was liberated. Laurence did not learn, until they were reunited in 1945, that she had a miscarriage in England; it was decided by SOE that this information should be withheld from him. He had received other news from SOE, on a regular basis, as to her condition and where she was living between surgeries to repair her legs.

A week after Giselle's escape from the Gestapo, Laurence had an opportunity to fulfill his orders to assassinate Krueger and exact his own revenge. On December 31, 1942, Laurence used his silenced gun to shoot Krueger as he was leaving what remained of Gestapo headquarters. The head shot was said to have killed Krueger and it was learned that his body was to travel to *Berchtesgaden*, his birthplace, by train. It was the last that anyone ever heard of Karl Krueger, the *Sadist of Croatia*.

For the next two years Laurence Penrose-Brooks continued his work with the resistance groups and was joined by an American, named Jonathan West, in a new plan to co-ordinate with the Allies and the planned invasion. On June 5, 1944, the largest amphibious assault in history took place with the invasion of Normandy. Both tactical and strategic surprise were achieved, much to the amazement of the Allied commanders. The only real setback occurred at Omaha Beach where American forces coming ashore were pinned down for much of the day and suffered tremendous casualties; however, they eventually got through and continued their march through France. The American forces broke out of Normandy in late July 1944 with Operation Cobra and by December 1944, Laurence was allowed leave to return to England to see his wife and get his new orders - France was liberated! He arrived in England on New Year's Day 1945 and saw his wife for the first time in two years. She was as beautiful as ever, but still walking with some difficulty even after her third surgery.

Laurence agreed to work as a translator with the reclamation project that returned precious works of art to their rightful owners and chose to be stationed in Paris where his wife would join him for his remaining tour of duty. It was a magical time when he and Giselle fell in love all over, again, away from the sound of guns and the stress of being found-out; it was probably the happiest time of their lives, with the exception of the birth of their son in April of 1946. Laurence remained with the military until 1950 and then accepted a teaching position at Columbia University, where he and Giselle would build a

new life in America.

Chapter Two

Vienna, Austria
June 15, 2005

Anthony West arrived in Vienna, just three days after the shooting of Laurence and Giselle Penrose-Brooks. He was exhausted after the rushed travel of the last two days, but did not want to waste a minute; lives may depend on his finding the answer to the reappearance of the *Sadist of Croatia* and his attempt to kill an old, harmless couple trying to live out their days on beautiful Lake George.

Simon Wiesenthal was known world-wide as the Nazi hunter. He had played a large part in the capture and rendering of eleven-hundred people to face justice for their atrocities during the war. He was an old man living out his days in his adopted country of Austria, in the city of Vienna.

Although the world-wide headquarters of the Simon Wiesenthal Center was in Los Angeles, Wiesenthal's small office in Vienna, known as the *Jewish Documentation Center*, was where Wiesenthal culled and analyzed mounds of documents and information captured from the Nazis and/or forwarded to him by his international network of friends, many of them World War II veterans and even, occasionally, former Nazis with a grudge to settle against a former cohort. This was where Anthony hoped there might be some useful information about Karl Krueger, the *Sadist of Croatia.*

Simon seemed delighted to see him despite his failing health, "How good to see you, my friend," he began after a firm handshake, "what can I do to help, Anthony?" West had told him on the telephone of the shooting of his old friend and his wife. "Do you really think that this shooting has something to do with the Nazis? How?" Anthony was about to respond when a housekeeper appeared with coffee and a Viennese torte. She served both and disappeared into the kitchen.

"Do you know the name Karl Krueger," West began?

"Ah, the *Sadist of Croatia*; indeed, I do. He was killed by a British agent in the winter of 1942. I remember reading the account in the archives." Anthony marveled at this old man's incredible memory for details. "How can he have anything to do with this shooting?" he finished. "He isn't dead, Simon. That British agent and his lovely wife are the victims of this shooting. The wife, Giselle, saw Karl Krueger three days ago in a lake resort community in northern New York, where they have built a retirement home," West finished.

"Not dead?" Simon queried. "I have heard nothing about this

man for over sixty years and you tell me he still lives?" He seemed stunned. "The *Sadist* still lives?" he reiterated. "My Godt," his accent grew thicker, "your friends, they will live?" he asked.

"Yes, Simon, they will recover, but they are still in danger from this man. There were no further attempts when I left them, and I have a guard outside their hospital room, but I must discover why they are a threat to him. Why didn't he just disappear, again; could it just be a revenge thing?" he asked.

"I think not, Anthony, too dangerous. As you say, he could have just disappeared, again. There is more to this. We must know what it is, we must!" he stated emphatically.

"Laurence Penrose-Brooks was the British agent who believed he had killed Krueger in late 1942. Word was spread around *Grenoble* and *Lac d'Annency*, where Penrose-Brooks was billeted, that Krueger's body was being sent to *Berchtesgaden*, for burial, where he and Hitler became fast friends before Hitler's rise to power and the creation of the Nazi party. I know that he was one of Hitler's closest, but somewhat secret friends and advisors, but that is all that I know," West stated. "Do you not think it strange," West continued, "that Krueger would have been pulled away from the French Alps, after the attempt on his life? It was a hot bed of resistance, much to the credit of Penrose-

Brooks, but the German reaction to an attempt on the life of an SS officer, especially a close ally of Hitler, should have resulted in more serious reprisals and a further increase in the German presence, but this did not really happen in this case. There were reprisals, but not to the degree one would have expected. Any ideas?" West asked.

"It seems they were trying to play-down the attention focused on Krueger, I wonder why?" Simon mused. "We must go digging, my friend. There must be something in the archives that can point us in the right direction. I have documented orders from Hitler, flight schedules, pay records, munitions inventories, there must be something! Finish your torte, it is especially good, today, and then we will roll up our sleeves, as you Americans say, and see what we shall see," he finished.

Wiesenthal and West had been working all afternoon before they found anything relevant to Krueger. "Here!" exclaimed Wiesenthal. "In January of 1943, just three weeks after the attempt on his life, Krueger had orders, from Hitler himself, to go to Rome by train to accompany a shipment of ten crates. This must be it, Anthony, a special mission ordered by Hitler, himself!" he exclaimed. Simon handed the document to Anthony and although Anthony's German was a little rusty (it was twenty years since he had been the CIA's station chief in

Berlin) he had little difficulty understanding the letter:

> 12 January 1942
>
> This letter authorizes *Oberstleutant* Karl Krueger to receive every aid, he so requests, in completing a special assignment ordered by me. This includes, but is not limited to staffing and the commandeering of transportation vehicles to travel to Citte del Vaticano with 10 crates of materiel.
>
> By My Hand and Seal,
>
> Adolf Hitler

"I think you are right, Simon, but what do you think was in those ten crates; looted artwork?" he queried.

"It seems a likely scenario," Wiesenthal agreed. "Anthony, are you familiar with some of the recent accusations against the Vatican Bank and its activities during World War II?" Simon asked.

"Only generally. I know that some feel that they were much too accommodating to the Third *Reich*," he responded.

"Oh, it was much more than accommodation,' Simon began; there is clear and convincing evidence that the *Instituto per le Opere di Religione* (IOR), commonly called the Vatican Bank became Hitler's personal banker. There have been a number of suits filed in recent years. Did you know that a Franciscan Order is accused of playing an active role in the governance of the *Jasenovac* concentration camp in *Croatia*?

"I have heard those rumors," West replied.

Just then West heard a telephone ring in another room and Wiesenthal left to answer it and returned momentarily. "It is for you, Anthony; it is Penelope with some bad news," he stated in a lowered voice. West rushed to the telephone, "Penny, what has happened?"

"A man dressed as a monk visited my grandparents room and attempted to inject something into my grandfather's IV tube. He was stopped, just in time, by the security guard, but it was a very close call. He was arrested and is in police custody. Could you arrange for additional guards?" she finished.

"I will do so immediately, Ms. Brooks. Tell your grandfather that I have a clue that I will be tracking down and I will let him know what I find. Ms. Brooks, I would like to e-mail you what I have found, to-date, and send material as I discover it. In case something happens to me, I would like you to have this information, in addition to my son, if that is agreeable?" West concluded.

"Of course, my personal e-mail is *pbrooks@gmail.com*, I will look forward to seeing what you have uncovered," she said.

West left Wiesenthal to go to Germany and, eventually, went from there to Spain to interview the only surviving SS officer who accompanied Krueger on his trip to the Vatican. Simon Wiesenthal died, peacefully, in his sleep, on September 20, 2005. Anthony returned for the funeral and had made arrangements with his son to pick him up at JFK; he was going home with a most incredible story.

Anthony West's concern and need to e-mail documents to Penny Brooks was prescient, he was fatally shot as he made his way through the arrival terminal at JFK to meet his son. The perpetrators were described as monks.

Chapter Three

New York City
September 26, 2005

Penny accompanied her grandfather to Anthony West's funeral. He left Lake George against all medical advice; he was still receiving physical therapy three times a week, but seemed to be doing well, otherwise. Her grandmother was still protected by four security guards at the chalet.

Penny had studied the documents that Anthony had e-mailed her, but she still wasn't sure what it was all about. A man named Krueger seemed to be at the heart of the mystery and a secret trip that he had made to Vatican City in January of 1943; the same man who was behind an attempt on her grandparents' lives.

Anthony's only child was a handsome young man about Penny's age. Her grandfather told her that he was a brilliant lawyer, working at the prosecutor's office in New York City. He was at the airport meeting his father when he heard the shots ring out. He made it to his father's side before he died and was, at least, able to say goodbye. Her grandfather had been terribly shaken by Anthony's death; he felt

responsible because he had been working at her grandfather's behest when he was murdered.

The funeral was large; Anthony had made a lot of friends in and out of government. Even the vice president was in attendance. Robert West, Anthony's son, and his uncle were the only living relatives. Anthony's wife had preceded him by five years after a long bout with uterine cancer. It wasn't until they returned to Anthony's brownstone, after the internment, that Laurence Penrose-Brooks finally had a word with Robert.

"Robert, I am so sorry. Your father was working for me when he was murdered. I cannot help but feel responsible. He was a dear friend, I should not have placed him in harm's way," he finished.

"Mr. Penrose-Brooks, I knew all about what my father was doing for you. Please do not feel responsible. He had not been so alive, so invigorated since my mother's death. He was doing what he loved to do and he was determined to get to the bottom of the attempts on your life and I think he did. He handed me a sheaf of documents from his breast pocket just before he died. He said the answer was in those documents. Obviously, I haven't had time to study them, but I will. If you could stay overnight, perhaps we could get together tomorrow and I will give you my thoughts on the documents. I will look at them in the morning. How about we all meet for lunch, say one o'clock at the

Waldorf?" he finished.

"That would be most agreeable. Thank you, Robert, for your kindness," Penrose-Brooks said.

Robert was already seated in the dining area when Penny and her grandfather arrived. He stood until they both were seated, " I could use a drink, will you join me?"

"That would be lovely," said Penrose-Brooks. Robert caught the eye of a waiter.

"I'll have scotch, neat," ordered Robert, "what about you, Ms Brooks?"

"Make mine scotch and soda on the rocks," and her grandfather had his straight on the rocks. While they were waiting for their drinks, Robert demonstrated his no-nonsense style and began:

"My father had been re-tracing the footsteps of a man known during the war as the *Sadist of Croatia*, an *Oberst* Karl Krueger. I understand you knew this man, Mr. Penrose-Brooks?" he looked to my grandfather.

"Please call me Laurence, it will save time. Yes, he was an *Oberstleutnant* when he came to the French Alps, where I was billeted at the time. That is where I met my wife. She was tortured by this man, and I thought I had killed him," he finished.

"Yes, my father gave me a brief overview before he left for

Wiesenthal's funeral. Apparently this Krueger was called away from medical leave in the French Alps to go on a special mission for Hitler. My father was able to get his hands on a number of documents that seem to show that this Krueger was sent on a super-secret mission to Vatican City. There is a document in this file that shows he was given *carte blanche* to undertake this mission and a copy of a telegram from Krueger to Hitler that states that he met with the secretary of state of Vatican City and reached the agreement that Hitler wanted. My father met with the only surviving SS soldier who accompanied Krueger on his mission and he states that Krueger had the secretary and the pope trembling in their shoes. He also states, with certainty, that Krueger sank a briefcase in the *Chiemsee*, a lake in Bavaria before he disappeared. He never saw him, again, before or after the war ended," he seemed to wind down.

"The Vatican?" queried Penrose-Brooks. "Of course we know that they accommodated the Nazis. I read a few years ago that there have been lawsuits, especially by Croatians who believe that the Vatican was the recipient of their entire treasury when the war ended. Do you suppose that's it? Neither my wife, nor I, had even the remotest thing to do with Yugoslavia. But, we Brits often thought that the Vatican may have been the recipient of stolen artwork in exchange for assisting some of the *ratlines* that were formed to get Nazis out of

Europe as the war was winding down. It must be something along those lines, don't you think?" he asked of Robert.

"Perhaps that's part of it, Laurence, but what about this briefcase sunk in the *Chiemsee* on the return trip from the Vatican? Clearly, something of great significance was in that briefcase. What became of Krueger for all the years until you saw him just a few weeks ago? My gut tells me that Krueger has been living here under a new identity and he does not want us to look for him to expose that new identity. He wanted to close the book with you and your wife. I doubt that he is worried for himself, he's an old man, but perhaps his family, his children?" he finished with a question mark.

Just then an attractive young man stood at Robert's elbow and cleared his throat to catch Robert's attention. Robert looked up and the young man said, "Robert, I was sorry to hear about the death of your father, please accept my condolences. Do we have any clues as to who did this dastardly thing?" he asked.

"Thanks, Tim. I haven't checked with the office, today, but the two monks seem to have fallen off the face of the earth. But, as soon as a clue pops up, I'll track it down myself, you can take that to the bank!" he said. The young man shook Robert's hand and moved away from the table.

"That was Timothy Witten, the son of Senator Witten, he's also with the prosecutor's office. There is talk, at the office, that Senator Witten is going to make a bid for the White House in 2008," he said.

"Robert, I would be happy to assist you with your investigation; I have taken an extended leave of absence from the newspaper and want to get to the bottom of this, my grandparents are still in danger," Penny filled the pause in conversation.

"I am well aware of your excellent credentials as an investigative reporter, Ms. Brooks. If I can think of anything, I'll certainly let you know. I need a little time for everything to sink in, but I have cleared my schedule, at the office, and I will be heading this investigation. It's no longer the sighting of a wanted war criminal and attempted murder, it is now a murder investigation involving my own family and in my bailiwick and I will be damn sure that if this character is behind my father's death, he will be brought to justice and I have the power of the prosecutor's office behind me."

Penny accompanied her grandfather on his train ride back to the Rensselaer station where she had left her car and drove the 50 miles back to Lake George. Laurence found flying to be too hectic at his age, and he loved the train; he liked to see the countryside on the ride north. Except for the stiffness in his shoulder that therapy was supposed to cure, he was doing remarkably well since the shooting. Her grandmother was also well, but she was constantly fearful something was going to happen; she slept very little and it was beginning to show. Penny was determined to use her own investigative skills to bring an end to this nightmare for her grandparents. She would stay the weekend with her grandparents, study the copy of the documents that Robert had given her that Anthony West had given his life for, but then, she would head back to the city where she intended to dog Robert West until he allowed her to join the prosecutor's investigation.

She was at his office, waiting for him, bright and early Monday morning. She saw him as soon as he got off the elevator, "Good morning, Robert. I hope you got some rest over the weekend," she said although he looked as handsome as ever. He was tall, dark and handsome, with brilliant, intelligent, warm, blue eyes. She knew he wasn't married and wondered if he had a girl friend; she didn't remember seeing him with anyone who seemed special at the funeral or internment.

"Good morning, Ms. Brooks. Yes, I was exhausted and slept nearly the whole weekend. Are you back to the city for an appointment?"

"Yes, with you. Robert, I need to help with this investigation. I know I am a little pushy, but I think I could be of help to you. My grandmother hardly sleeps, she's waiting for another attempt on their lives. She has more than earned her peace in her old age; this is so unfair! I can't stand it! I have to do something!"

"I understand, Penny. I really do. Let me have the morning to put together a few ideas as to a plan of attack. Let's meet for lunch, at the Hyatt, and we'll go from there, OK?"

"That sounds good, it'll give me time to empty my suitcase and do laundry. What time?"

"Let's say 1PM."

"Good. See you then." Penny had been living out of a suitcase for weeks, it would be good to see her apartment, the one she was given by her grandparents when they moved to Lake George. It was a two-bedroom condo on Fifth Avenue and something she could never have afforded on her salary and trust fund put together, but now it was hers! It was a secure building, with a security guard and special key cards needed for the elevator and to enter a unit in the building. Her grandparents felt more at ease knowing that she lived in such a secure building in the heart of the city. They worried over her safety especially after a couple of explosive investigative reports that she had done for the paper.

Robert was surprised at how much he was looking forward to his meeting with Penny. She was a drop-dead, gorgeous woman, who didn't seem to flaunt it. She inherited her grandfather's height, she must be 5'10", but she had her grandmother's French features, with dark hair and enchanting, aquamarine eyes that seemed to change color from blue to green. She could have been a model, he thought. When he first laid eyes on her he felt his heart skip a beat. Despite the grief he was still feeling at the loss of his father, thoughts of Penny kept intruding. He wondered if she was in any kind of committed relationship.

Robert was the first to arrive, again, and stood as Penny made her way to his table up the steps to the Hyatt's version of a garden-on-the-park, although they were looking down on a steady stream of people on 42nd Street. Robert was already sipping his scotch, neat; it took a few minutes for the waitress to arrive and Penny ordered a glass of wine.

"You look lovely, Penny, that sweater matches your eyes," Robert spoke, first.

"Thank you," Penny smiled as she remembered how frantically she went through her closet looking for the exact sweater to wear. She was saved from saying more by the waitress who came to take their order. As soon as she left, Robert began his analysis of all that his father had told him and of the documents his father gave him. Penny could understand Robert's success at the prosecutor's office; he was a critical thinker and not afraid to have an original thought.

Robert opened a notepad and said, "I have a few ideas, let's call them talking points; let's see what you think:

1) I do believe that Krueger is living in this country and has made some kind of reputation for himself that he does not want exposed. Given his advanced age, I think he does not fear for himself, but a family relationship that would be ruined by his exposure. Perhaps a son or daughter is in some position of power.

2) Krueger possesses a manuscript powerful enough to blackmail the Vatican; it is clear to me that he sank it in the *Chiemsee* and if he emigrated to this country, I'll bet my bottom dollar that he brought it with him or has retrieved it sometime over the years.

3) Either monks or people dressed as monks were involved in the attempts on your grandparents and my father's murder. Under ordinary circumstances, I would say that murderers were dressed as monks and not believe that monks would commit murder, but if the Vatican has been blackmailed ever since the war, who knows? Perhaps there is a renegade faction of the Vatican government that *would* commit murder. Assuming this to be the case, for a moment, my father's death must mean that they are protecting Krueger's identity. My father was getting too close to the real story. Perhaps Krueger put pressure on the Vatican to do something when he was first exposed by your grandmother. In conclusion, I think we have to take a two-pronged approach to get to the bottom of this: try to uncover Krueger's

present identity and try to find out what he has that could cause monks to become murderers," he seemed to conclude on cue, the waitress arrived with their lunch. They ate their broiled fish, both lost in thought.

Penny spoke, first, "Do you think he came here after the war ended or after he finished his assignment to Rome?"

"An assignment involving a manuscript that could bend the Vatican to Hitler's will would be worth its weight in gold. Hitler is gone and perhaps Krueger has the only copy, Hitler's probably destroyed with him and perhaps one of them had the wisdom to foresee the failure of the Third *Reich*. My guess is that Krueger got out as soon as he could, with or without Hitler's permission," Robert finished.

"It would be my plan of attack to study the entry logs from Ellis Island," stated Penny, "to zero-in on a one to six month time period from the date of Krueger's assignment to Rome, do you agree?"

"I do," agreed Robert, "and I think we need to take a trip to Spain to see this character that my father last visited. He is said to be the only surviving SS officer of that trip, by train, to Rome. I suggest we do that, first, and then come back and tackle the Ellis Island records. How soon could you be ready to leave?

"I just need to repack my suitcase, grab my passport and I'll be ready," Penny stated, "where in Spain are we going?"

"The *Costa del Sol*," it should be nice with a lot of the summer tourists gone," he replied, "perhaps we'll have an opportunity to take a dip in the Med; bring a bathing suit, just in case."

Chapter Four

The plane trip was uneventful, which was a good thing in the age of Al Quaeda and/or its sympathizers. Spain had foolishly bowed to the terrorists in its 2004 elections, after the attacks on its transportation system; her grandfather had been livid, but people do foolish things when they are scared.

Robert and Penny decided to stay in *Malaga* although *Mijas*, where *Herr* Erhard Schmidt lived, was still an hour's drive west of *Malaga*. They took the Mediterranean Expressway AP-7, N-340 until they reached *Benalmadena* then picked-up the A-368 to *Mijas*. The road paralleled the coastline for much of the way; it was a truly beautiful, peaceful drive and Robert handled the rental car with ease. Schmidt's little stucco house had recently been whitewashed; it sparkled in the morning sun. They had called the previous evening to confirm the 11AM appointment. Although Schmidt was in his eighties, he moved like a man in his fifties as he led them to a table and chairs on the west side of the house. There was a pitcher of lemonade with glasses and a tray with rolls, cheese, sausage and olives for a late morning snack. It was October 1, but the sun was hot, the temperature already 85 degrees.

"I was sorry to hear about the death of your father, Mr. West. He seemed like a very nice man. We spent an afternoon, together, going over old war stories. He had a special interest in a Major Krueger. Is that why you have come?" he queried in English.

"Yes," answered Robert, "he died before he could tell me what he learned from you."

"I do not know what became of Krueger; I do know that after the assignment to Rome, in which your father was interested, he returned to *Berchtesgaden* and I never saw him again. Those of us who traveled to Rome with him were disbursed to all different battle lines. We were told to never discuss what went on at the Vatican with anyone," he said.

"Will you tell me what you told my father about this assignment? What was the purpose of your trip to the Vatican?" Robert asked.

"The war is long over Mr. West, and those who have kept their secrets in the hope that there will be a Fourth *Reich* are fools. I do not believe another *reich* without Hitler is possible. Hitler had the ability to convince people that he could give Germany back its pride after the humiliation of the First World War. He lost his way and lead Germany down the wrong path. It was the so-called *Final Solution* that destroyed the soul of Germany. Many thought the reunification of the two Germanys would give it back its soul, but the strain on Germany's economy has failed to accomplish that end."

"What about Rome?" prodded Robert.

"We took crates of confiscated valuables to Rome to be held by their bank. Krueger had a manuscript that had something in it that scared both the secretary of state and the pope. Somehow, Hitler and Krueger were able to blackmail them. I am quite sure that Krueger sank a briefcase in the *Chiemsee* on our return trip to *Berchtesgaden.* He stopped the train, left with a silver briefcase and returned two hours later without it. He headed toward the lake and was freezing when he returned. The lake had not frozen over; the temperatures had been too mild. If Krueger is alive, he is probably still holding this manuscript over the head of every pope," Schmidt concluded.

"Do you have any idea what the manuscript is about?" asked Penny.

"Yes and no," began Schmidt. "I was told by one of the other SS guards, who served in *Croatia* with Krueger, that Ante Pavelic's people found a religious object in one of the mines in *Croatia* and turned it over to Hitler as part of an agreement to let Pavelic rule *Croatia*. I do not know if this is true, but it sounds very plausible. Hitler had more than a passing interest in religious objects; I have been researching the man for many years in an attempt to understand what drove him to some of his actions. You see, I am the author of many works about the war, you may know me better as Richard Wellington." "Of course," spoke Penny, "several of your works were in my father's library. I inherited them and have even read a couple of them. I thought you were British?"

"My mother was British and I honor her by using her maiden name as my *nom de plume,"* he replied. He continued, "There are many things that the world still does not understand about Hitler and we study such things, do we not, so that we do not repeat our mistakes? I believe that whatever Ante Pavelic gave to Adolf Hitler, it confirmed his world view for Germany and for his own role as a world leader. If, as I believe, Hitler got his hands on the Holy Grail or the Ark of the Covenant, he could, indeed, bring the catholic church to its knees; especially if what has been taught about the object is not accurate or, at least, changes church teachings significantly. I learned, since your father's visit, that there is a scientist in Germany who worked on a secret project involving the discovery of an unusual device in the former Yugoslavia. I was planning to travel to Germany to see him next week-Monday; perhaps you would care to join me?" he asked.

"I think that would be a great starting point, *Herr* Schmidt," said Robert. "We will return to *Malaga*. I assume you will be flying?"

"Yes, I will meet you in *Malaga*, at the airport on Monday at 9AM for the 10:30AM flight, if that's agreeable?"

"That is fine. Thank you for your hospitality, *Herr* Schmidt," said Robert. They all shook hands and Penny and Robert headed back to *Malaga*.

"How nice! We have five whole days to relax in the sun," said Robert as they made their way to the highway heading east.

"Shouldn't I go back to New York," Penny began, "to start the search of records at Ellis Island?"

"That would be the logical thing to do," stated Robert, "but I would rather you keep me company, here, and I would like you to go to Germany with me; your German is a lot better than mine."

"Since two of the five days are a weekend I probably wouldn't accomplish that much anyway. I guess I could keep you company," she smiled.

Robert reached over to take her hand and it was if a jolt of electricity went through her body. She had never felt that spark before and wondered if Robert felt it, too. It was as if he were reading her mind, "I don't know if you felt what I felt," he began, "but, I confess that I am falling in love with you."

"I think I am, too," Penny stumbled, "with you, I mean." Robert looked away from the road to Penny and their eyes met and stayed for what seemed too long for someone driving, "You'd better watch the road, Robert!"

"Oh! you're right; but it is a real challenge with you sitting right next to me!"

The days flew by and Penny confessed to Robert that she had never been so happy in her life. They swam in the Mediterranean Sea and baked in the sun on its sandy beach. It wasn't until their final night at *Malaga* that they both succumbed to the desire that had been building since they returned from *Mijas*. They had arranged for connecting rooms and at 12AM, Penny opened the door to Robert's room and made her way to his bed. She gave herself, completely, for the first time in her life. She knew that she would never be able to live without him.

Schmidt was late. It was already 9:30AM with no sign of him. Boarding time came and went; Robert went to a telephone to call, but there was no answer at Schmidt's house. Departure time came and went. They decided they had better drive to his house to see why he was a no-show for the flight to Germany.

No one answered their knock, but Robert found the door was not locked. He stepped into the foyer and called Schmidt's name. No answer. They both moved through the house calling his name. Robert made it to the bedroom before Penny and found what he had feared; Schmidt was dead and it was no peaceful crossing into another world. Schmidt's throat had been garroted. Schmidt's suitcase was on the bed and partly packed for the trip, but someone had been able to sneak up behind him with a garrote. He had fallen forward as if kneeling to pray, with his forehead actually touching the bed further opening the large gaping wound. Someone, clearly, did not want Schmidt to go to Germany. Robert's Spanish was much better than his German; he went to the telephone to call the authorities. While waiting for the police, Robert made his way to a desk he found in a small room next to the bedroom. There was an envelope with a name and number written in block letters; Robert was pretty certain it was the name and number of the scientist in Germany (he was certain it was a German calling code) who they were supposed to meet that day. He slipped it into his pocket. As a prosecuting attorney, Robert knew that he should not touch anything, Schmidt's house was a crime scene, but he feared they would never find his father's killer without interviewing this man in Germany, without knowing what this manuscript was all about.

It was nearly three hours before the police confirmed that

Robert was who he said he was and confirmed that they were booked to fly to Germany. Schmidt's plane ticket was in his inside jacket pocket. Robert provided contact information, but informed the police that they would, probably, be spending a few days in Germany. He told the police that Schmidt had provided contact information for the man in Germany and Penny and he intended to reschedule the meeting with him. It was true in a round-about way.

The drive back to *Malaga* was rather somber, not even the breathtaking views could lift either one's mood. When they reached their hotel room, they agreed that Penny should place the call to Germany.

"*Doktor* Goldberg, I am sorry to inform you that *Herr* Schmidt was murdered very early this morning. Robert West and I were to accompany him to see you for an appointment, today. My name is Penny Brooks." "He was murdered, you say?" asked Goldberg.

"Yes," Penny replied, "but Mr. West and I would still like to meet with you before we leave Europe."

"It is not safe, Ms Brooks! Surely you can see the danger for you and myself? I am an old man, but I prefer to die peacefully in my bed. What is it that you want to know? We can discuss it on the telephone; it is safer for everyone," he said with certainty.

Penny turned to Robert and whispered, "he is afraid. He wants to do this on the telephone." Robert nodded his head in agreement; best to get the questions answered as soon as possible, he thought.

"*Doktor, Herr* Schmidt told us that you worked on a special project for Hitler involving some kind of device found in Yugoslavia. Can you tell us what that device was?"

"Ms. Brooks, this can be a very dangerous thing for you to know! Are you sure that you want to have this knowledge? It has been a terrible burden for me for many, many years! It was only my scientific knowledge that kept me, a Jew, from going to the gas chamber, but sometimes over the years, I have thought that might have been better than living with this knowledge. So much of what I believed as a scientist and as a Jew has been challenged by the discovery of this object. It is very hard to comprehend how it will change one until you come face-to-face with its inescapable truth. Why must you have this knowledge?" he queried. Penny explained about the attempts on her grandparents' lives and the death of Anthony West and, now, Erhard Schmidt. She told him about Krueger and the manuscript.

"*Ja,* I see that it is best that you know, but we cannot cover all the information on the phone and if you come here, I may be the next to die. Perhaps an old man can show his skill with the modern contraption called a personal computer with scanner, *Ja*? Give me the fax number where you are staying and I will fax the information you need. I do not have a copy of the whole manuscript, but I have all my notes from this project. I gave fake papers to the Nazi bastards who were sent to collect my notes when the project was finished. These will do, *Ja*?"

"That would be wonderful, *Doktor*. Here is the hotel's fax number."

"*Sehr gut*, but you may not think it is so wonderful when you understand what you have, Ms. Brooks. Well, good luck to you. It would be best if you do not try to contact me, again. I may be able to live another year or two, *Ja*?"

It took nearly 2 hours for all the pages to print from the hotel's fax machine. Robert grabbed the sheaf of papers and headed back to the room to study them with Penny. After nearly three hours they both looked at each other, somewhat bewildered and Robert spoke first. "Is this possible? How was it possible for this to remain a secret? Who was the first person who decided that we did not have the right to know this? It's unconscionable!"

"It must have begun with the very early priesthood," spoke Penny, "when this device was lost, don't you think? How could they perform these sacrificial ceremonies and not tell the people that the reason for these *ceremonies* no longer existed? It is the most egregious cover-up imaginable! No wonder the Vatican buckled under Hitler's blackmail threat," Penny said. "Do you think it was brought to Yugoslavia by one of the Knights Templar as suggested in Goldberg's notes?" Penny wondered out loud. She continued to muse, "No wonder *Doktor* Goldberg said his life wasn't the same after working on this project; both the Jewish and Christian religious articles of faith are affected by this discovery. Wow, what an uproar this is going to cause!"

Robert replied, "I wish we could get our hands on a copy of the whole manuscript. I think the only safety, for everyone involved, is to get this published as soon as possible. Once it is in the public domain there would be no reason to kill over it. Do you think you could put together a newspaper article with Goldberg's notes?" he queried.

"How could I begin to corroborate the information? Perhaps Goldberg would see the wisdom of publishing, but I would never get anyone from the Vatican to participate; I doubt that I could even get an interview with anyone at the Vatican once they know the subject matter," Penny said. Just then there came a knock at the door. Robert answered the door and there was a gunshot; he fell to the floor as Penny rushed to his side, but the shooter was still there. Someone, dressed as a monk, raised his gun, again, and shot Penny. She collapsed on top of Robert.

Chapter Five

Berchtesgaden, Germany
January 15, 1943

"*Heil* Hitler," saluted the young soldier serving as Hitler's receptionist at his mountain retreat at *Berchtesgaden*.

"*Heil* Hitler! I am *Oberstleutnant* Karl Krueger, I have an appointment with the *Fuhrer*," he saluted. "Just one moment and I will announce you," he stated while checking his list of people scheduled to see the *Fuhrer* that day. He returned just a couple of minutes later and led the *Oberstleutnant* to a large room with a huge fireplace. Hitler was seated next to the fire. It was mid-January and cold in the large, open-ceilinged room.

"Karl, my friend, how are you?" he asked as he stood from his comfortable seat. "I see from the bandage on your head that it was a very close call. Perhaps the French Alps was not the best place to recuperate. Those damnable swine!"

"I was lucky this last time," *mein Fuhrer*, "I would like to have stayed and routed out these damned resistance fighters! They are playing havoc with our supply lines," he remarked. You know that we caught that French skier? It was her British agent-lover that shot me," he stated.

"*Ja*, there is a great deal of work to be done there," but I need you for another assignment after you have a had a few days to rest. You are the only one I trust with an assignment of this magnitude."

"May I ask, *mein Fuhrer*, where this assignment will take me?" asked Krueger.

"I guess there is no harm in whetting your appetite," he smiled, "you will be traveling to Rome, first class, of course! Now go, give my warmest regards to your mother, find a nice girl to bed and come back rested and ready to be surprised," he winked.

Krueger was usually amused by Hitler's little secrets and surprises, but after a hard year in Croatia, and two gunshot wounds in the last three months, he was all out of patience. He wasn't even sure he had the energy to woo a nice girl into his bed. He had seen how other SS officers took whatever girl they wanted through rape and the *Utashe* were even worse; he saw the gang rape of many women. He knew it would have been suicide to try to interfere, but he did not socialize with those animals. It was disgusting! He may be called the *Sadist of Croatia*, but he was doing his job shipping people off to prison camps and shooting or whipping those who couldn't follow orders, as an example, but he did not crawl in the gutter with the riff-raff.

On March 30, 1941, Hitler issued a directive, *Operation Enterprise 25*, to destroy Yugoslavia as a military power and sovereign state and on April 6, 1941, the German *Luftwaffe* attacked Belgrade, killing between twelve and seventeen thousand people, but not one bomb was dropped on *Croatia*. Ante Pavelic returned to govern the new State of *Croatia* after twelve years in Italy. On April 30, 1941, Pavelic called for the "purification" of *Croatia* by eliminating "alien elements." Serbs and Jews were required to wear armbands. At the end of April, Pavelic was granted a private audience with Pope Pius XII and on June 6, 1941, Pavelic met with Hitler, who signed-off on a resettlement plan and counseled Pavelic to pursue a "fifty year plan of intolerance." This alliance lead to the deaths of 750,000 Serbs, Jews and Gypsies at the hands of the *Utashe* (*Croatia's* brutal army) whose tactics caused some German commanders to pale.

While this was the historical and public agenda for this meeting between Pavelic and Hitler, something of far greater reaching significance took place, in secret, that would lead to a new partnership between the Third *Reich*, Pavelic and the Vatican. Pavelic turned over to Hitler a large crate that accompanied him on his trip to Germany. It was quickly turned over to a group of scientists, from many different disciplines, who were given one year to study its contents. It took only nine months; the scientists had succeeded in reverse-engineering the device found in the crate. It was more exciting than he had ever hoped! Hitler was ready to test the device in the Fall of 1942. It was the predicate for events that happened during the war that were never satisfactorily explained. As agreed, the original device would be returned to *Croatia*, and remain under the dual guard of a Franciscan Order and the brutal *Utashe*. Hitler knew he now possessed the power to blackmail the Vatican See. They would be eating out of his hand; he didn't trust the Swiss, completely; he needed another banking partner for special funds, and he just found it! Krueger was the right man for this job; he was a personal friend whose loyalty to Hitler was unquestioned and he could handle himself in any situation.

Krueger arrived at 8 AM Monday, as ordered. He was sent into Hitler's large office, where he found a table laden with pastry and coffee. Hitler hadn't arrived, yet. He poured himself coffee, and took a piece of *apfelstruddel.* He had just finished the pastry when Hitler arrived. He jumped to his feet and shouted, "*Heil* Hitler," with spine and right arm ramrod straight!

"Relax Karl, this is just going to be an informal meeting between us, Old Friend," he said as he closed the door. "You are going to be told something that only a handful of scientists know in Germany. It is the purpose of your trip to Rome and you will be my sole and secret legate to the Vatican See. You will find it hard to believe what I am about to tell you, but I assure you it is the absolute truth," he said.

Krueger listened for the better part of two hours and then was handed a bound manuscript and told to read it while Hitler left the room to attend to some other matters. It took another two hours to read the manuscript and when Karl was finished his head was spinning. He could hardly believe what he was reading. He was raised a Christian, but whatever beliefs he had had fallen by the wayside. A lot of what he read certainly made some sense and he could certainly see that the Vatican would do whatever it could to ensure that this manuscript never saw the light of day. My God! What a stroke of luck for Hitler!

Hitler returned and handed Krueger a letter of authorization to commandeer a train and to pick whatever staff he chose to guard the ten crates of artwork, gold and diamonds and other precious stones that had been stolen from the Jews and other misfits in Germany - hundreds of millions of dollars worth of valuables. Karl understood that he wasn't to give the secretary of state of the Vatican See the opportunity to refuse this new banking partnership. If there was any difficulty, Krueger was authorized to shoot to kill, until the Vatican relented.

"There are three copies of this manuscript, Karl: I have one, you are to give one to the secretary of state of the Vatican and the last, and this is very important, Karl, you are to bury your copy, and a crate that goes with it, where no one will ever find it, but you. You know we have buried many documents and valuables in lakes throughout Germany and Austria. You choose the spot. Tell no one, not even me. If this all falls apart, someday, should we be overrun by the Allies, you are to use that document and crate to begin again. You will have all the funds you need, at the Vatican Bank, to start the Fourth *Reich*, if need be. After this mission, you will be retired as an *Oberst (Colonel)*. I want you to leave Germany and the war. You are my ace-in-the-hole. Go to America, perhaps. Start a family and when the time is right, use the Pavelic legacy to start again. I will not see you, again, my friend. When you have finished this mission, contact my secretary. There will be instructions and all the documents that you need to build a new life." They shook hands and embraced and Krueger saluted smartly, clicked his heels and left Hitler's mountaintop retreat.

It took Krueger a week to pick fifty of the SS's best and bravest to accompany the train to Rome; he wanted to arrive with overwhelming force. He also outfitted the train with snow removal equipment.

The train would leave *Berchtesgaden* and travel through the

Tyrol* to *Innsbruck*, which he was dreading. There had been several weeks of heavy snow and it was not unusual for an avalanche to bury the train tracks, either natural or man made. Stopping to remove snow was dangerous in that part of Austria. They could be picked-off one-by-one by the resistance while trying to clear the track. If they could make it through the *Tyrol*, Krueger was confident the trip down the center of Italy's boot and then the crossover to the west coast and the *Citte Del Vaticano*, the Vatican City, would be uneventful. The trip could be made in a matter of hours or a matter of days, so he arranged to have the train outfitted with food supplies, a chef and service staff to feed the fifty soldiers and himself. He thought about taking some girls along, but he didn't want that getting back to Hitler, so he didn't. The soldiers could relieve their tension when they got to Rome.

They had made it to *Innsbruck* without incident, but just outside the city as they made the turn south, they could see that the track ahead was buried in a mountain of snow. However it was caused, it would take hours to clear the track. The temperature had plummeted when they reached the heart of the *Tyrol* so Krueger divided the soldiers into 5 groups who would work in two-hour shifts to remove the snow. He couldn't afford to let them get too cold or too tired or they could be days moving the snow. The first two shifts were marked by considerable progress, but just as the third group started their shift,

two men were shot dead before Krueger could order the group back inside the train. The rifles were disbursed; each soldier was picked because they were expert marksmen. The hail of bullets went on for a half-hour before Krueger halted the firing. It became clear that the resistance was trying to get the soldiers to use up their ammunition and attack during the approaching nightfall. Krueger took an inventory and was concerned that a third of their ammunition had been used in that first half-hour of conflict. They would have to be a little smarter. He was a little afraid to use larger weapons; they might bury themselves in another avalanche. They couldn't precisely pinpoint where the bullets were coming from. Should he sacrifice a group to draw fire to try to locate the resistance group's position? He would need all hands if they decided to attack when it was dark. He decided to wait. Let them sacrifice their men! Half the men were told to get some sleep while the other group took up their positions along the 5 cars. Four men were sent to protect the locomotive.

It was all quiet until about 2 o'clock in the morning. Several of the windows were shattered by a hail of bullets, but no one was seriously injured, thank God! Everyone took up their rifles and their positions, but were told not to shoot until they had someone in their sights. Krueger sent 5 men to crawl to the roof of each car to keep it free of anyone brave enough to crawl aboard. Those men could only have gotten into position when he heard gun shots, but could not see anyone around the train. "Five men to the south side," he heard shouted, "one-hundred feet!"

"Let them get closer!" he shouted. "Keep low and don't waste your ammo!" It was a few minutes later that he heard a rifle shoot.

"I got one!" came the immediate shout. "The remaining four have taken cover behind the snow pile, twenty feet ahead of the engine!"

"Group One take up positions outside, now!" Krueger shouted! Half the men exited the train. Minutes passed as Krueger feared someone getting close enough to destroy the locomotive. The silence continued for another hour and he knew the men outside must be freezing; it was time to rotate the team. "Group Two, outside to replace Group One!" It was a foolish time for the four resistance men to attack. They must have misread the activity from the train, thinking just some of the soldiers were outside and moving back inside. All forty-eight men were outside as the four resistance fighters stepped away from the snow pile and started shooting. They were all killed in a matter of seconds, with only three of Krueger's men injured.

The soldiers began digging snow again at daybreak and the train was underway about 11AM. Coffee was served and a meal was prepared by the kitchen staff and served at 1PM. All the men were fed and rested as they began the trip down through Italy. There were no more incidents and they arrived in Rome at 7PM. Hitler's secretary had arranged for Krueger and his men to stay at the Hotel Savoy on the *Via Veneto.* Hitler did promise first class! His men deserved a hot bath and meal and they would get a good night's sleep in a luxury none of them had seen since the beginning of the war. The Italian Gestapo would guard the train until the meeting, which was scheduled for 10AM with the secretary of state of Vatican City. The train would go from Rome's city terminus right into the heart of Vatican City on its own rail system. Half the men would guard it and the other half would accompany him to his meeting. He would not disappoint Hitler; the Vatican would be eating out of his hand before he left Rome! He couldn't wait to see some of these arrogant bastards brought to their knees and he was just the man to do it!

The secretary of state stood as Krueger was shown to his private office. "Ah, *Oberstleutnant*, how was your journey?" he asked.

"That is of no consequence!" came the retort. The secretary looked at his shoes as Krueger continued. "This manuscript will take you about two hours to read. I and my men will wait outside until you have digested it. It will do you no good to attempt to destroy it, there are copies. When you have finished, send your assistant to get me. Is that understood?" he demanded.

"It is perfectly clear, *Oberstleutnant*," replied the secretary.

"My name is *Oberstleutnant* Krueger! You will address me by my name in the future!" Krueger spat out.

"My apologies, *Oberstleutnant* Krueger," cowed the secretary. Krueger turned and marched out of the room with twenty-five of his men in two columns at his heels. Two and a half hours passed and the secretary's assistant had not returned for Krueger and his patience had expired. "Let's go men," Krueger spoke to his men, "we have some convincing to do." They arrived back at the secretary's office with no sign of him or his assistant. "Open fire, men, kill anyone in sight and destroy those fancy chandeliers up there," he pointed to the hallway ceiling. The gunfire should have awakened the dead, it echoed off the narrow hallway walls, and several chandeliers had fallen to the floor before Krueger spotted the secretary making his way toward him, with his assistant distinctly using the secretary as a shield.

"Stop shooting!" Krueger shouted to his men.

"I apologize for being tardy," cowed the secretary, "I had to see the pope for a moment before calling for you. It was not necessary to destroy those priceless chandeliers," he whined.

"Let's get this straight, Mister Secretary," he began, "you don't call for *me!* You were to send your assistant to *get* me. You were given a timeline. If I can read that manuscript in two hours, you should have been able to do the same. If you needed to see the pope, I should have been informed of that fact. Now, you and I will meet, in private, to conclude our business, is that clear?" he finished.

"We will meet, in private, of course, but we can go no further until I hear from the pope. Do you understand? I cannot make a decision of this magnitude, I had to include the pope in this momentous matter. I outlined the material for him and he wanted to look at the manuscript, himself," he concluded. "I understood from *mein Fuhrer* that *you* would make this decision," began Krueger. "I do not like this change," he stated.

"Surely, you can understand the importance of this matter? I could not make this decision on my own. The wrong decision could change the future of the church. It must be the pope's decision," he finished and Krueger could see that his complexion was about three shades whiter than when they first met. Perhaps it was not so bad that he wait. Hitler having the pope's imprimatur would be even better than this greedy secretary's cooperation, who had demanded money for his assistance, "We will wait, here, until you hear from him," stated Krueger. It was an hour and a half later when the secretary was called to the pope's office and Krueger and his men accompanied him. Krueger decided not to insert himself into the conversation with the pope and it proved to be a wise decision. The secretary came out of the

pope's office shaken and far weaker than he entered.

"By the pope's authority, the Vatican Bank would be pleased to offer its services to the Third *Reich*. Please move your train to our railroad terminus to offload the crates you wish the Vatican Bank to take custody of, and in the future, you are to contact the Bank, directly, for whatever services you require. I believe this concludes our business," *Oberstleutnant* Krueger," he concluded. Krueger saluted an especially proud "*Heil* Hitler," turned and clicked his heels and marched away with his men in tow! He was ecstatic, he had not had to kill anyone. (Although that would not have bothered him, in the least, but Hitler would be pleased.) The men were given forty-eight hours leave in Rome and as requested, a telegram was sent to Berlin (where Hitler was supposed to be) immediately after the meeting at the Vatican. Krueger received a return telegram by the time he checked out of the Hotel Savoy, two days later, that read:

> **"25 January 1943**
>
> **Well done, Oberst Krueger!**
> **Congratulations on your pro-**
> **motion. Please follow my**
> **previous instructions.**
>
> **Best of luck, my friend,**
>
> **Signed, Adolf Hitler"**

The return trip to *Berchtesgaden* was uneventful, with the

exception of an unscheduled two hour stop, during the night, at the *Chiemsee*, a lake between *Rosenheim* and *Berchtesgaden*. Only *Oberst* Krueger got off the train at this stop, carrying an aluminum metal container, and no information was given to any of his men except to stop anyone who came near the train and hold them until he returned. A middle-aged man appeared just as Krueger was returning from the lake and he was questioned, extensively, by Krueger and, eventually, let go. He was the owner of a local *gausthaus*, at the lake, and returning home after cleaning-up after his late dinner shift.

Krueger picked up his documents at *Berchtesgaden* on January 27, 1943, and made his way to Amsterdam where he would be taken, by boat, to England to catch a ship leaving for Boston on February 20, 1943. No one questioned that he was a Swiss banker heading to New York City to work at the new American branch of his Swiss bank.

Chapter Six

At first, Krueger was bored working under his new identity. After the power and the action of a soldier in Germany during the rise of the Third *Reich*, banking was a mind-numbing activity. It took nearly a decade to grow comfortable in his new role. He found a nice German girl that he married on February 4, 1948 and she bore him a son on March 4, 1950. By 1955, Krueger, now known as Karl Witten, was a senior vice-president of his bank. After his marriage, he had really applied himself. The Third *Reich* was long defunct; his old friend, Hitler, had committed suicide and the Americans were now ruling the world. The 'cold war' between America and the Russians was something that Hitler had predicted when he first learned of Russia's agreement to join the Allies during the war. He said that when the Americans had a glimpse of communism, up-close and personal, they would find it far more objectionable than Hitler's philosophy of government. If Hitler had not been worn-down by the war in Russia,

they might have gone all the way! Oh well, that was past and his present may seem a far cry from his glory days, but the future held a great deal of promise.

In 1960, Karl Witten decided it was time to go back to Germany and retrieve the manuscript from the *Chiemsee.* He wanted it closer to him.

Karl Witten's son was the tender age of ten when he first saw the stomping grounds of his father's native Germany. He could not tell his son about his glory days and the day he had the pope of the growing Catholic Church eating out of his hand. What a power rush! He would live it all, again, if he could. Someday, he would tell his son. His son would be the new leader of the Fourth *Reich*. There had been many comments, over the years, by his German wife that suggested it would not be so traumatic for her to learn that Witten was one of the darlings of Hitler's SS. She felt that Hitler had been on the right road until he became hungry for land that he should not have tried to steal for the Third *Reich*. Krueger/Witten remained silent on the issue.

On July 9, 1960, Karl Witten and his family arrived in Munich, Germany. Immediately, Karl felt an ache in his heart for the land he had had to leave. Could he leave it, again? Karl's wife, who he loved deeply, was born in Munich, so the trip was supposed to be an opportunity for her to visit the land and city of her birth. Karl could not, yet, share the pain in his own heart as he saw sights emblazoned in his own memory. He rented a car to drive his family to the heart of Bavaria, his beloved *Berchtesgaden* and the *Cheimsee*. They stayed at a new hotel called the *Zimmer Frei* and could only travel to the "Eagle's Nest," Hitler's mountaintop retreat by bus. It was their first stop before backtracking to the *Chiemsee*. It was a sight to show their son because of its historical importance, but Karl's throat began to close up as the bus neared the "Eagle's Nest." Here, he had embraced his old friend for the last time. As they got off the bus, Karl turned away to wipe a tear from his eyes.

"Oh Karl, what a beautiful view! Have you ever seen anything so beautiful in all your life!" she exclaimed with the excitement of a child.

"No, my dear, I have not. It is wonderful, isn't it?" he remarked. "Let's go inside to see where Hitler issued many of his orders. Karl Jr, come here! We are going inside." Karl's son came to his father's side as they moved to the steps of Hitler's mountaintop retreat. Karl's mind went back to the last time he ascended those steps; to get the passport and documents that Hitler had prepared for him and his flight to America so that he would not be killed in the war. He did not want to leave Germany. He was not afraid of dying, but he had to admire Hitler's long range view. The Third *Reich* went down in flames, but Hitler had made provisions for the Fourth *Reich* and he was supposed to be its leader; but Karl knew that it would be his son that would fulfill Hitler's dream. He would be groomed to be a senator from the great state of New York and then, perhaps, a president of the United States of America. The Fourth *Reich* would be a stealth *reich*; it did not have to reach pre-eminence through the bloodshed of the old days; the new, one-world order could be gained through control of the United Nations - that was Karl's long-term plan for his son. Karl could see his son being educated at Harvard and with the funds available through the (IRO) Vatican Bank, he could finance young Karl's track to control of the United Nations by a path through the White House.

"Here," spoke Karl, "this was Hitler's office," he spoke to his wife and child.

"How do you know that, dear?" asked his wife. "Have you been here before?" she asked.

How should he answer, he wondered? "I was here, once, before we met." He left it at that, as did she; but she did give him one of those looks that he loved; like, 'you know more than you are saying; you can't fool me, mister.'

Liesl was a beautiful woman, with the blonde hair and blue eyes of an Aryan. Her heart was made of gold, with great compassion and passion. He never knew that sex could be such a wonderful experience. She made him hunger for the end of the working day and coming home to a woman who could totally possess him. She made him forget that year in *Croatia* when the great power the soldiers wielded corrupted the meaning of sex. He learned how to love and to make love to this beautiful creature. He was still as deeply in love with her as the day they met. Each time they made love, she took more and more of his soul and washed away the stain of the war. She owned him. She could look deep in his eyes and he became weak in the knees with the mere memory of the last time they made love. He was her slave and delighted to be so. She was truly an angel sent from god; sent to punish him with kindness.

The tour of Hitler's mountaintop retreat did not take long. They would have five days at the *Chiemsee* to relax and for Krueger to recover the manuscript and then on to *Salzburg* to the music festival that Liesl begged to attend and then home.

The *Chiemsee* is a Bavarian, idyllic lake at the foothills of the Alps; famous for its association with King Ludwig and his *Herrenchiemsee Castle* that looked a lot like the *Versailles Palace*. To keep the lake idyllic and eliminate the noise from the many tourists it draws, only small electric boats, with blue canopies, can now be rented at the lake.

On their third day at the lake, Krueger decided to make his move. Everyone was fast asleep, at 2AM, when he left the small hotel

and stole one of the boats and carried the scuba gear that he had rented the previous day. The case was dropped at the deepest part of the lake, nearly 74 meters deep. He used a compass to find the exact co-ordinates where he dropped the hermetically sealed case seventeen years ago. He prayed that no one had found the case during some underwater exploration. It took him a half hour to find the case and his heart was pounding as he released it from beneath a couple of inches of muck. When he broke the surface, he had to swim twenty feet to the boat. On board, he used a hotel towel to clean the case and made his way back to shore. He was relieved to see that no one was about, no one had heard him leave. Thank god for those quiet engines! He stripped-off the scuba gear and put his pajamas on and returned to his room; both his wife and son were still fast asleep thanks to a day of swimming and sunbathing. Everyone was already two shades darker than when they had left home. He went into the bathroom and closed the door. He soaked the towel in hot water and finished cleaning the case and dried it. It looked brand new! He would tell his wife that he bought the case to carry important papers to and from work. He had to get rid of the towel! He remembered seeing a laundry chute down the hall so he left, as quietly as he could, and got rid of the towel. He put the case under the bed and crawled into bed next to his wife; she didn't stir.

Karl had peeked inside the case while he was in the bathroom and found the manuscript as new as the day he placed it inside; in the hermetically sealed case it had not yellowed in the least. He was too excited to get back to sleep although he was exhausted after his dive. He worked-out at a gym to keep his body trim, but his wife's wonderful cooking made it a constant struggle; after all, he was 42 years old. Karl slept-in that morning; told his wife he had had trouble sleeping (the truth!) and sent her and his son down to the lake to swim. He joined them at one o'clock for lunch and spent the afternoon just dozing in a lounge while Liesl and Karl Jr. swam. They had one more day at the lake and would then drive to *Salzburg* for the music festival. It was there that his new life came into jeopardy.

It was Hitler's secretary, the man who had handed his new identity papers to him almost eighteen years ago. He literally bumped into Witten. "Watch where you are going, sir!" admonished Witten. "*Oberst* Krueger, how nice to see you, again, I am truly sorry," he said without an ounce of concern. "I'm sorry, sir, you have me confused with someone else. My name is Witten," he countered. The man began to pale as he realized what a mistake he had made. How could he have been such a fool? Karl realized the problem immediately; the man was drunk!

"I am so sorry," he said, "please excuse my clumsiness." He

bowed his head to Liesl then turned and walked away. Karl knew he could not let this man live. He could spoil all the plans he had for his son to make a career in international politics. If he could not control his drinking, he would always be a threat to all his plans. He might even attempt blackmail, the poor fool. Krueger remembered the man's name; it was uncommon enough to hope he could find his name in the telephone directory.

As soon as they were back at the hotel, Witten searched the directory and found only one name that had to be his man. He was living in *Hallein*, a small town just across the border from Germany into Austria and only about 15 miles from *Salzburg*. He would wait until his wife and son were asleep and drive to *Hallein*. He could easily be back in an hour, if things went well.

Witten was surprised that the lights were still on at 2AM, when he drove up in front of the house. He knocked on the front door and it was answered within a few seconds. He was delighted to see that the man was dead drunk; it should make his mission easier. He wanted to make it look like an accident.

"Ah, *Oberst* Krueger, I knew that was you at the festival," he managed to get out of his mouth! "Have you come to have a drink with me?" he finished.

"Why not," Krueger said, "is your wife asleep?"

"She divorced me and took the children ten years ago. I seldom see them," he said in a whine. He turned to walk toward the bar and Krueger asked if he could use the bathroom. He quickly found what he needed; a small, stand-alone heater used to warm the bathroom on cold mornings. Although it was July, the authorities would find that the man was too drunk to know what he was doing. It would be just a tragic accident. He started filling the sink and closed the door to return to the bar. "Let's have that drink, now, and then I must return to my wife. I just wanted to let you know, that if you see me in the future, you must address me by the name I have been living under for the past seventeen years - Karl Witten and, *Herr* Lorenz, you must do a better job at controlling your drinking," Witten admonished.

"I am sorry," he began, but never had a chance to finish. Witten grabbed the little man and started dragging him to the bathroom. He opened the bathroom door and found what he expected; a sink overflowing. He turned around, so he would not have to enter the bathroom and shoved Lorenz to the bathroom floor and stepped away from the bathroom door with the heater he had left on top of the toilet seat cover that he could reach from the doorway of the small bathroom. The extension cord was stretched to its limit. As Lorenz struggled to get to his feet, made nearly impossible in his drunken state and a tile floor under an inch of water, Witten turned on the heater and then tossed it, as gently as he could, on top of Lorenz, to break its fall. As Lorenz pushed it off him to the floor, his body began to jerk as the electricity flowed into him. It only lasted a minute or two and Lorenz was dead. He left the water running, turned and left the house. It was easier than he had ever hoped (so he thought). He was back at the hotel an hour and ten minutes later. Liesl stirred as he crawled into bed and spoke his name, but fell right back to sleep.

He was still asleep at 10AM, when there was a loud knocking at the door. He saw that Liesl and Karl Jr. were in the dining area where they had already eaten breakfast that they had ordered from room service. He put on his robe as Liesl opened the door and Karl was dumbstruck to hear the man identify himself as a police detective. How could they possibly know, wondered Karl? His heart was pounding as he relived the wiping of everything he had touched at Lorenz's house. There were no fingerprints, he was sure!

"*Herr* Witten, I must ask you to accompany me to headquarters to answer questions regarding the death of Erik Lorenz," he said. How could he know, pondered Witten?

"Officer, I do not know an Erik Lorenz. There must be some mistake," he said, "my wife, son and I just arrived in *Salzburg*, yesterday, to attend the music festival. We are scheduled to leave for home, that is New York City, this afternoon. Why is it you think I have anything to do with this man's death?" he queried.

"Because of this," he held out his hand. Karl nearly fainted when he saw his wallet in the detective's hand, "this was found in the bathroom of *Herr* Lorenz, where he was electrocuted by a heater in room flooded by water that had not been turned off in the bathroom sink," he said, "it had apparently fallen out of your pocket when you wrestled Lorenz to the floor, it was beneath his body," he finished.

Karl had a lot of practice thinking on his feet and was ready to respond when Liesl came to his rescue. "Karl!" she exclaimed, "It was that man at the festival! The drunk that bumped into you. I'll bet he picked your pocket!" What a bright woman he married!

"Of course! Detective, there was quite a disturbance last night when this drunk literally collided with me. He almost knocked me off my feet. If you speak with the staff at the refreshment lounge, they will confirm what I have said. You will also hear from your medical examiner that this man was very drunk. I will certainly comply with your wish to come to your station, but I had nothing to do with this man's death," he finished.

"If I can confirm what you have said in the next few hours, I will ask, only, that you just come to the station to give an official statement. Perhaps you could reschedule your flight for this evening, and we will hope it is all cleared-up by then. Please stay close to the hotel until you hear from me," he finished and turned to walk away.

"Papa!" exclaimed Karl Jr., "how could they believe that you could do such a thing?"

"They do not know me, Karl; they reached their conclusion based on incomplete information. I am confident that it will be cleared-up this afternoon. Don't look so worried, son. Everything will be alright," he finished. He turned to his wife and she slid into his arms. Nothing more was said. "I will grab a shower and dress and we will go to the hotel's sidewalk cafe. We still have traveler's checks in the hotel's safe so we don't have to go hungry until they return my wallet!"

It was one o'clock as they went out the hotel's front entrance and walked to the sidewalk cafe. "What a beautiful day," he exclaimed, "please do not let this business spoil your appetites!" They all decided on the *wiener schnitzel* and it was wonderful. No one appeared to be waiting for their table, so they stayed and lingered over coffee; Karl stayed to read a newspaper while his wife and son decided to go to the hotel's gift shop. It was about three o'clock when the detective made his way to Karl's table. "*Herr* Witten, I have good news! We have confirmed the altercation at the music festival and *Herr* Lorenz's blood work did show that he was terribly drunk, three times the legal limit. The death has been ruled an accident. We are sorry for the inconvenience we have caused your family, but you do understand that we must inquire?"

"Of course, Detective Kunzel. Shall I come with you, now, to make my statement?" Karl asked.

"That would be most helpful, *Herr* Witten."

"Just let me speak to my wife, she is in the gift shop." The detective followed him to the front entrance of the hotel. His wife looked up as he approached her. "It has been ruled an accidental death. I am going to the station, now, to make my statement. I shouldn't be long."

Liesl looked incredibly relieved. She gave Karl that incredibly beautiful smile, that could light up any room, and he kissed her on the cheek, then left to meet the detective. What a close call, Karl mused to himself; Liesl had been instrumental in this quick outcome.

"Karl," Liesl spoke as the luggage was being tagged at the airport, "I don't remember that silver case, is it yours?"

"Oh, I forgot to mention it, with all the commotion. I bought the case at the *Chiemsee*." She had not seen Karl load the luggage into their rental car when they left the lake for *Salzburg*. "It is a secure case, with a combination lock, that I can use to carry confidential documents that I need to bring home from work. It was not terribly expensive, and you just can't beat German engineering," he said. She said no more and they walked to their departure gate with boarding passes in hand.

The flight home was uneventful and soon they were back to their normal routines. Karl carried the silver case back and forth to work until he could determine the best place to store it. He was on his way home from work, one day, when he saw a nearly identical case in an upscale store on Fifth Avenue. What luck! He bought it immediately and asked them to hold it until morning. He knew Liesl would miss the case, if he stored it in the bank vault; his dilemma was solved!

The following summer Liesl asked if they could spend two weeks of their summer vacation at Lake George. Her brother had bought a motel at the lake and he raved about the beauty of the Adirondack region; he said it made him think of the foothills of the Bavarian Alps - even the *Chiemsee*. It gave Karl an idea. He knew that there could be questions, someday, about leaving personal property in the bank's vault; perhaps moving it from the *Chiemsee* to Lake George was poetic? He would take the case with him and decide when he saw the lay-of-the-land.

The region was all that Erik (Liesl's brother) bragged about and more. The motel that Erik purchased was right on the lake, with fifty units, and would prove to be a gold mine based on the thousands of people invading this small resort town. They took their son to visit many of the historical places from the French and Indian war and then to a large amusement park that Karl Jr. loved. He begged to go on a huge roller coaster that had them all turning green by the time it was over. By the second week, Karl knew this was the place to sink the case, again, and he knew that investing in Erik's motel would be a good move. He knew from Leisl's remarks that Erik was looking for some additional capital for renovations and Karl decided he would invest, personally, in this project. It was a sound move, financially, and it would tie him to the lake. Erik wanted a half a million, Karl would provide double that amount; he wanted to ensure the success of Erik's venture. He had that amount, himself, but it was time to tap the Vatican Bank. He did not want them thinking they were off the hook. He would send a telex as soon as they returned to the city.

Chapter Seven

Vatican City, Italy
July 9,1961

Although there had been a change in popes, the same secretary of state remained in the administration of the Vatican government. It was Tuesday, July 9, 1961, that he saw the first communication, since the war, regarding the ten crates of valuables that the Third *Reich* had placed with the Vatican Bank. He received a copy of a telex sent to the bank, by Karl Krueger, the *Oberstleutnant* (who had been so obnoxious 18 years ago) for his approval. Krueger, now known as Witten, required that the contents of those crates be liquidated over the next few months. He wanted ten million dollars in cash and letters of credit for the remainder. It would be enormously dangerous to liquidate the artwork, but perhaps it could be done through private dealers. The jewels should not be so difficult, they could be removed from their settings. He really had no option but to approve the request in the telex. He initialed it and sent it by courier to the bank.

It was six months later before he heard anything more about the contents of the telex. He received an informational memo from the bank that the artwork had been sold in four lots, to some of the more unsavory contacts of the bank, who were private collectors, in the amount of seven-hundred fifty million dollars and the jewelry sold for another two-hundred fifty million dollars. The secretary of state was shocked! One billion dollars to that obnoxious twit! What could he do? Could he risk causing the man any trouble? He had a copy of the manuscript that could bring down the church, if its contents were ever made public. Does anyone else know about this manuscript?

Chapter Eight

New York City
June 25, 1975

Karl Witten Jr. graduated magna cum laude, first in his class at Harvard Law School and distinguished himself as editor of the 'Law Review.' He had already accepted a position with the prosecutor's office in New York City. Karl Sr., now 58 years old, had purchased a small private bank with the proceeds from the Vatican Bank liquidation of the Third *Reich's* ill-gotten assets. He tripled the assets of the bank in the fourteen years he had been its president and sole stock holder. He had acquired prime real estate in Manhattan, maintained a robust stock and bond portfolio, and was known throughout the city as the best currency arbitrager in the business. He worked, on contract, with several brokerage houses to buy and sell currencies for their institutional clients.

Before taking up his position at the prosecutor's office in September, Karl Jr. wanted to spend the summer backpacking through Europe with two of his friends. He would meet his parents in Munich in mid-August and they would spend a few days together at the *Chiemsee*. August 15th came and Karl Jr. did not appear. Liesl and Karl Sr. were deeply concerned. Their son was a very responsible person; something was wrong. It wasn't until early the following day that the bad news came by telegram:

> "Mr. Witten:
>
> Karl was kidnapped yesterday evening,
> as we left the hotel, by two men dressed
> as monks. What should we do? Stay
> in *Grenoble*? Would these people
> contact us? Or, you?
>
> Please call us at 011-33-04-555
>
> Brad Merriweather
> Robert Wells"

Monks? Karl's mind was working in hyper-drive; what could this mean? Was the Vatican involved? Were they dumb enough to make this kind of stupid mistake? He no longer *needed* the Vatican; did they really think they could use his son as leverage to get the manuscript? Liesl was beside herself, but Karl was steaming beneath the surface. It was late afternoon when he received the telephone call: "Mr. Witten, if you wish to see your son again you will leave the manuscript, in a brief case, at the foot of the steps of the *Villa Borghese* in Rome, on August 18 at 11AM. Your son will be released unharmed if you do as you are told. Do you understand?"

"Yes, it will be as you say."

Oh, God, thought Karl! He was going to have to tell Liesl all about his Nazi past and about the manuscript and crate! How could he? She worshipped him. They were still lovers; despite the passage of time they had never grown bored with each other. She was proud of the life Karl had made with her and their wonderful son and daughter. They owned a luxury condominium building on Riverside Drive and lived in the Penthouse. An idea was forming in the back of his mind; maybe there was a way to do this that would not require a full confession to his family.

He told Liesl the content of the telephone call.

"What is this manuscript that you have that they want?" she asked. "Liesl, over the years I have invested in rare books and documents. Some of the documents were owned by Adolf Hitler. I recently acquired a document, actually a manuscript, from his estate that has something to do with a discovery made by Ante Pavelic and a Franciscan Order in Yugoslavia during the war. It seriously challenges the interpretation of biblical literature by the Judeo-Christian Church. This must be what they want. I will have to fly to New York to retrieve the manuscript and then to Rome to exchange it for our son. I think you and Annamaria should stay here in case there are any further instructions. Do you understand, *Liebchen*?"

"Yes. Then you think it is the Vatican that ordered the kidnapping of our son?" she asked.

"I am certain of it," but it will all be over in three days. Try to calm yourself. Annamaria, please take good care of your mother while I am away," he finished. Before he boarded the plane, he sent a telegram to the secretary of state of the Vatican, demanding that his son be released unharmed, or he would release the manuscript to the media. The flight to JFK would have been unbearable without the three glasses of wine that he drank to calm his nerves. His backup plan was already formulated, if the Vatican did not respond to his telegram.

There was a response from the Vatican on his desk when he made it to his office at 8AM. He had only had three hours sleep and nearly exploded when he read the telegram:

> "Herr Witten:
>
> Please believe me when I say that
> neither I, nor the Vatican government
> knows anything about the kidnapping
> of your son.
>
> His safe release will be in our thoughts
> and prayers.
>
> Signed,
> Cardinal Carlos Berloni
> Secretary of State
>
> Citte del Vaticano"

Is he calling my hand or could he be telling the truth, thought Witten? Could the monk's clothing used by the kidnappers just be a ruse? Would the Vatican play 'chicken' with something that could spell its demise? Who else knew about the manuscript? If not the Vatican, it might have come from Pavelic's people, but how would they know he had a copy of the manuscript? That could only have come from Hitler, and he was long gone. Did he tell anyone else? Could this just be a way for some group to find out if I *did* have a copy? So many doubts. Perhaps his backup plan was really the best way to proceed.

He flew *Alitalia* to Rome and arrived the morning of August 17, a full day before the exchange was supposed to take place. He slept until late afternoon, showered and dressed to have some dinner. He hadn't eaten much in the past two days and was beginning to feel the pangs of hunger. He decided to leave the hotel on the *Via Veneto* and stroll to a restaurant near the *Villa Borghese* where the exchange would take place in the morning. He found a four star restaurant and had a sumptuous meal of Veal *Marsala.*

He finished dining and as he left the restaurant he spotted two monks and a young man getting into a limousine; that young man was his son! At least he knew that his son was unharmed. He knew it would be hopeless to get a cab in time to chase after the limo and it might endanger his son. He returned to the hotel slightly relieved that he had seen his son. It was time to call Lee (as she preferred to be called for the past fifteen years). Annamaria answered the phone and he told her he was in Rome and wished to speak to her mother.

"Oh Karl, I am frightened out of my mind! Have you heard anything more," she asked?

"No further conversations, my dear, but I saw Karl Jr. just a little while ago. As I came out of a restaurant near where the exchange is to take place; he was with two monks getting into a limo. I wasn't able to follow, but he looked fine, Lee. I have the manuscript and everything will go fine, tomorrow. I'll have our boy back and we will see you for dinner tomorrow," Karl stated with certainty.

"Please Karl, give them whatever they want! I cannot lose my son!" she said and Karl could hear the tears in her words.

Karl had not remained in contact with any of the Nazi organizations that helped to relocate officials of the Nazi regime. He had made his own way in life, but he needed to hire some thugs to teach these people a lesson; they should not mess with Karl Krueger! He made a few telephone calls and eventually found the men he was looking for and went over the plan in very great detail. There could be no mistake.

It was Friday morning, 10:50AM, when Karl entered the *Villa Borghese* carrying a silver briefcase. He saw no sign of the men he hired, but that was the plan. He spotted two men, dressed as monks, and his son moving toward him. One walked up to him and he held out the briefcase for the man to take. He walked back to his partner, who opened the briefcase, nodded and released Karl Jr. who rushed to his father's side. The two monks walked away. Karl was not an openly affectionate man, but he hugged his son and they turned to walk back to Karl's hotel.

Two hours later there was a knock on the hotel room door and Karl Sr. answered the door. He was handed the same silver briefcase that he had handed to the two monks. Karl removed a fat envelope from his inside jacket pocket and handed it to the man at the door who said, "Everything was done as you requested." Nothing else was said. Karl returned to his son and resumed packing for the trip back to the *Chiemsee*. A mere ten thousand dollars, he thought, to get back the photocopy of the manuscript he had made in New York City, and the death of two kidnappers. Not a bad day's work and the message was very clear to whoever was behind this scheme.

Chapter Nine

Karl Witten Jr. had distinguished himself during his ten years at the New York City prosecutor's office so when he decided to run for attorney general he had some name recognition. He was easily elected and served three terms as attorney general. His three senatorial races were more contentious; Democrats were determined not to lose this seat, but his father's money bought television spots that the Democrats could not afford in the last few weeks of the campaign. It made all the difference.

Karl Witten Jr. was, now, an attractive fifty-six year old three term senator from New York State. Although his conservative views were far right of most of the country, he had quickly learned the political game of staying in the middle-of-the-road when it came to campaigning. He was now being prodded by both his parents and the movers and shakers in national politics to run for the White House in 2008. His wife of thirty years felt that he had a good chance of winning, but felt that Karl should make the decision and said she would support whatever he decided. Their son, Timothy, was doing well at the New York City prosecutor's office (following in his father's footsteps) and their daughter, Isabella, was teaching law at Georgetown.

Karl Witten Sr. still went to his bank, occasionally, to survey the small kingdom he had built. It was actually run by a very competent staff of twenty-five people. At eighty-eight, Karl was still quite young looking and had never had a sick day in his life, with the exception of an occasional cold. Liesl had aged well; Karl was still extremely proud to have this beautiful woman on his arm as they dined in all the finer restaurants in the city. Karl was one of the wealthiest men in the country, although not in the same class as a Bill Gates. He was prepared to start his son's bid for the White House with a war chest of a hundred-million dollars and would provide more, if needed.

As Karl Sr. watched the activities of what were called Neo-Nazis; he was reminded of the days when Hitler's clarion call brought all the riff-raff into the movement; most of them were just out-of-work thugs in search of someone to blame and beat. That had nothing to do with the philosophy of the Nazi party or Hitler, although he had developed an inordinate hatred of the Jews. Karl had thought a lot about that over the years and concluded that Hitler was jealous of their wealth.

Most went into the professions or became successful businessmen and women. Jewish families handed down great wealth from one generation to the next and were able to give their children the best education. These were opportunities that Hitler never had and he let his jealousy get out-of-hand when he held great power. He also believed that Germans were descended from a superior race of beings.

Even at this late date, most people in Germany and around the world did not understand the meaning or the impetus behind Hitler's concept of a master race. It came from a deeper meaning than the mere belief that a certain archetype (Aryan) was the best representation of a true German; it came from the myths and legends that informed Hitler's belief. When Hitler served in World War I, he experienced a gas attack and was temporarily blinded; during this time he believed that he had a sort of spiritual experience. It quickened Hitler's quest for esoteric knowledge which he came to believe was behind this experience. One of the earliest influences on his thought was Lanz von Liebenfels; he claimed that "Aryan" peoples originated from interstellar deities who bred by electricity, while "lower" races were a result of inbreeding between apes and humans; von Liebenfels advocated the mass castration of racially "apelike" ethnically inferior, sexually active, men. The 1905 work, *Theozoologie oder die Kunde von den Sodoms-Afflingen und dem Gotter-Elektron,* had a huge impact on Hitler and some of these ideas were acted out during the Nazi "purification."

Hitler began to believe that some of the Judeo-Christian articles of faith and some of the miracles of both the old and new testament books of the BIBLE were really acts performed by a more advanced civilization that had visited earth from another civilized planet somewhere in the vicinity of our solar system. Karl knew these were not the ravings of a mad man; others throughout recent history had reached the same conclusions, but when Ante Pavelic handed over the device found in Yugoslavia, it was no longer just a belief. Hitler's hatred of the Jews grew more strident when he concluded that the ancient Jewish priesthood was responsible for the greatest cover-up in all of human history; that they possessed knowledge that they withheld from the rest of civilization.

Karl Sr. knew when the war was over that there would be no Fourth *Reich* that would simply be a continuation of Hitler's later years. The Nazi party could not survive after the atrocities committed in its name. There may be a lot of Germans that were still nationalistic, but no one, of his or his son's generation, would trust another leader as they had trusted Hitler to give Germany back its pride after the humiliating World War I defeat. Many felt a renewal of pride with Hitler's successes, but few knew how much Hitler had lost his way until he committed suicide. Some knew of the atrocities committed in the name of war, but most Germans did not. The generation living through the war had mixed feelings about the war, but the second generation since the war were ashamed of Germany and lived under a cloud of guilt. When the wall fell and the two Germanys were united and the economy began to bend under all the extra weight, some of those old feelings were stirred. It started just as it had sixty years ago: those unable to find work began to resent all foreigners in their country. Skinheads donned some version of the swastika and roamed neighborhoods looking for someone to blame and beat, but there was no one strong enough to lead Germany out of its troubles as Hitler had. Karl Sr. saw a Germany that had moved too far to the left; there was no way that he would return to get involved in Germany's politics. Germany would be forever stained by Hitler's solutions. Karl would content himself being behind the scenes of his son's political career that would, one day, make him the leader of a one-world government; a government that would be Hitler's delayed legacy.

It was not until Karl Jr. reached the age of twenty-one that Karl took him to the bank, one day, and sat him down to read the manuscript compiled by some of the greatest scientists in World War II Germany (some who escaped Germany and went to work for the

United States government). His son was shocked and wanted his father to publish the manuscript, it would be an immediate bestseller, but Karl Sr. said the time was not right. He wanted Karl Jr. to release the manuscript when he became president of the United States. It would give him more power than any man in human history, even Hitler! That same night Karl Sr. took the manuscript home; he wanted his wife to read it also. It was time to confess everything to Liesl and their children. Everyone came home on Sunday for the weekly family dinner. Even though the children lived away from home, it was still a family rule. Both the children lived within driving distance of their Riverside Drive home; all were supposed to come, including the spouses, and grandchildren.

That evening Karl Sr. told Liesl who he used to be. She was not the least bit surprised nor put-upon because he had never told her the truth. She was a German and lived with that same mixture of pride and guilt coming out of World War II Germany. She understood Karl's fear that his secret could inadvertently slip out of her mouth during their early years together. He no longer had that fear and wanted Liesl to understand why he had pushed Karl Jr. so hard. He would be the man to release this information to the public, but at a time when he had great political power. She agreed. It might just as well be at time that would help her son.

It was hot for early June and they had agreed, at the Sunday dinner, that everyone would join Karl Jr. at his campaign announcement at Lake George, New York. Karl Jr. had been invited to speak at a gathering to be held at the beautiful Sagamore Hotel. This would be where he would announce that he would be seeking the office of President of the United States. After the announcement, they would spend a week, all together, at the beautiful lake and take the great grandchildren to the Great Escape, where Karl Jr. had spent many summers in his childhood. Karl Jr.'s campaign manager would notify the media so that he would receive national exposure when he made the announcement, in time for the 6 o'clock news. It was the day his father had been planning for nearly sixty years. He would let nothing get in the way of this moment.

There were nearly twenty satellite trucks from all the broadcast channels, local channels, cable channels and even the foreign news outlets surrounding the Sagamore Hotel. The family had decided to stay at the hotel the night before the speech even though they would spend their week at the motel that was co-owned by Liesl's brother, Erik and Karl Sr. Karl Sr. had warned that it would be impossible to get through the mob on the day of the announcement; he was proven right. They simply went downstairs at 4PM, for the cocktail hour meet and greet part of the evening's program. They would dine on lobster tail and chateaubriand and then Karl's speech would follow. Both Karls and the speechwriter had spent nearly the whole day polishing the speech that Karl Jr. was about to give.

Karl Jr. was introduced by a local dignitary after the last waitress left the dining room and began his speech, "Good evening ladies and gentlemen. Before I speak the words you all came to hear this evening I want to describe a vision that I see for this country. It is a vision that departs from business as usual in Washington, DC. Our government has become so big that, in most circumstances, it is ineffectual. If you need a good example of what I mean, just look at your government's response to Hurricane Katrina. The left hand did not know what the right hand was doing and neither hand provided essential services for the communities affected by this disaster. No one seemed to be in charge, although everyone was purportedly working on the problem. That's because there is a large machine in Washington DC that gobbles-up tax dollars that are assigned for various purposes, but getting that money out and where it needs to go does not work. You have all heard the old adage, 'too many cooks spoils the broth?' In Washington DC, everything is management by committee, which is something of an oxymoron. When something goes wrong, as it invariably will, everyone in the committee points the finger at the other guy or gal. Nothing gets done, problems don't get solved. Everyone throws up their hands and decries the red tape as the problem and everyone puts their head down until the storm passes and goes right back to doing the same thing over and over again. This is not good government no matter what political party is in power. It has to stop. We have to redesign this machine that keeps gobbling-up our tax dollars, but does very little to serve our needs. This is not a matter of political philosophy, this is a matter of good principles of management. No large corporation in this country could function in this manner and no president should be expected to steer a ship of state when everyone else keeps trying to grab the wheel. We need to make fundamental changes in the structure and administration of our government.

In the weeks to come, I will describe this new vision with you. Most of you know that I am described as a fiscal conservative, but I'd like to take a moment to first explain why I am a Republican. I do not believe that a centralized government best serves the people. (In reality, Karl wanted a weakened federal government and presidency to suit his future plans.) The previous topic is a good example of the pitfalls of a centralized government; it becomes too big to function effectively and it costs too much to send all federal tax dollars to Washington DC and then turn around and send money back to the states. That process, alone, costs hundreds of millions of dollars (enough to pay down the national debt over ten years, or so) and often the money does not get back to the states in a timely manner. Simply by letting the states and communities keep that money, we solve their cash flow problems and they can better serve the people in their own communities and save an enormous amount of money in administrative costs. That's why I am a Republican. The Democrats want you to send even more money to Washington DC so they can think up more and more ways to spend it. The Democrats believe that you should give them *all* your money, accept a small allowance, and then let government meet all your needs. We know that we cannot depend on the wheels of government to do that, don't we? Big government is not very different than a fiefdom with its serfs who work for a king. The machine of a government is impersonal, but make no mistake, it still takes the dollars you have slaved to earn all year long, just like a king. This country was founded by a courageous group of people who refused to serve a king who stole the fruits of their labor and told them how and where to worship their God. We have made a mockery of their sacrifice by creating a *machine* worthy of a king! It is time to take this machine apart and build a better one.

Some have asked me, over the years, why I am not enrolled in the Conservative Party. The reason requires a long, hard look at the realities of American politics. Let's say that on election day we have a fifty-percent turn-out of the electorate in a three-way race for the presidency. That means that the winner of the election may have as little as 1/3 of the fifty-percent turnout or only 16% of the people have elected the President of the United States. Perhaps the electoral college will modify those percentages somewhat, but you get the idea. That is why I am against a third party candidacy. I do not believe that represents a clear mandate for a president. I believe that we should move to a program where every person, of legal age, is *required* to vote in a presidential election; it is a duty of citizenship. The rest of the world should know that a United States president truly represents the majority of his or her people. I do agree with some, in the conservative movement, who suggest we should move to a flat tax rate as soon as possible.

I announce, herewith, that I am seeking the office of President of the United States and as your president, I will work to strip away the bureaucracy that has come to enslave us all." There was a roaring, standing ovation. The news cameras were rolling and cameras were flashing. Rebecca, Karl Jr.'s wife, went to his side and kissed him and stood with her arm around his back. They were an attractive, photogenic couple. Their son, Timothy and daughter Isabella joined them, but Karl Jr.'s sister, Annamaria, her husband, Jeffrey, Karl Sr. and Lee remained at their table. Karl Sr. was filled with enormous pride; he was certain that his son had just begun the journey of his true destiny. He was certain that he would be visiting the White House in January.

Karl Sr. had agreed to go to the Lake George Arts Festival with his wife. They usually missed the festival because they visited the lake later in the season, usually in July. Karl Jr. and Rebecca were to spend the afternoon swimming and lazing in the sun with Annamaria and her husband, Jeffery. The grandchildren, Timothy and his girlfriend, Diane, and Isabella had their own rented car and were to go to one of the shopping malls. It would give Karl Sr. and Lee a chance to take a nap after visiting the festival. They all planned on going on the *Lac du Saint Sacrement* for the late dinner cruise.

Karl Sr. had about his fill of walking and was looking for Lee when he saw a woman staring at him. She stood stock still and just stared. Karl Sr. was beginning to feel uncomfortable when the woman turned to move away. She was walking with a cane and appeared to be a woman in her sixties. He was about to dismiss the whole matter when she turned, again, to look at him and he knew, in an instant, who it was. My God! Sixty years and she really had changed so little; still a beautiful woman looking twenty years younger than her age. That day came flashing back. He had gone to the French Alps to recuperate from a gunshot to the gut. He was grateful to get out of

Croatia. The bloodletting was out of control. He was no pansy but the *Utashe* and their knives, the hacking-off of body parts was too much even for him. After two months in the mountain chalet, he sought new orders from headquarters and was asked to check-in with Gestapo headquarters at *Grenoble* to see if he could help with the interrogation of an important prisoner; one who had a lot of information about the French resistance in the alpine region. It was the woman skier, *La Petite Papillion*. Everyone had been looking for her. She was tough. . . wouldn't say one word. Hitler was depending on him to crack her; after the second day, he knew she would never talk without a lot of inducement. He ordered a lead pipe be used on her legs; even if she never talked, she would never carry messages for the resistance again. The bastards got her out and bombed headquarters and then there was the attempt on his life the following day. What a mess! But, he was called away to *Berchtesgaden* and told to fake his death. One of the strangest requests he had ever received from Hitler.

What was she doing here, he wondered? Could she be living here? What if she connected him to Karl Jr.'s announcement at the Sagamore Hotel last night? Oh God! She could spoil it all! After sixty years, she could spoil it all! He wouldn't permit it! He would have to follow her, find out where she went, kill her if he had to. She would not deny him what he had waited for; his son was going to be the next president!

He saw the car that she had gotten into, a man driving, and quickly recorded the license plate number; his son should be able to use his influence, as a senator and presidential candidate, to get an address from the department of motor vehicles. Then he would come up with a plan. Who was that guy who wanted to be Karl Jr.'s bodyguard? He was a former Navy SEAL and an expert marksman; Karl has his application.

For two-hundred fifty thousand dollars, Mark Endicott had agreed to come to Lake George and kill the two people designated by Karl Witten Sr. The money was insignificant to Karl Sr., he would have paid many times that, if Endicott had asked for more. Endicott would arrive the following day and decide how to carry out the murders, without getting caught. He told his employer that it might take a day or two to do it properly.

When the first attempt failed to kill both people, Endicott agreed to stick with the mission until he succeeded. He was one of the best SEALS the Navy had ever created; he wasn't used to failure. He might be older, but he could still keep up with the newbies. He hated leaving the Special Forces, but his wife wanted him to find work that was less dangerous. Personal bodyguard to a presidential seemed a good spot for him. There was a little danger, but it wasn't the middle of Iraq with its guerrilla warfare. He had already served two terms there; he had done his part for his country. He was fifty years old, serving twenty-five of those years as a SEAL. His wife was right - it was time to get out.

Mark decided to wait until his quarry was released from the hospital, then he would blow up the damn chalet with both of them in it and be done with this mission once and for all! He was flabbergasted to read in the local paper that a monk had been arrested trying to inject something into the IV tube of Penrose-Brooks; old man Witten was not the only one who wanted the old couple dead. Who the hell were these people that everyone seemed to want dead? What did they know that made them such a threat?

Chapter Ten

Malaga, Spain
September 27, 2005

Robert West was in critical condition; he had been shot in the abdomen with several organs damaged by bullet fragments. He had lost a lot of blood and was close to death by the time he arrived at the hospital. Penny had been shot in the right collarbone, but there was a clean break; the bullet missed her lung by a fraction of an inch. She had lost a lot of blood and was in serious condition. The next twenty-four to forty-eight hours would determine whether they would live or die.

Penny was pretty alert when the surgeon came to visit the second day following the shooting. He spoke English, making his care of the two Americans that much easier. She listened to what he said about her condition, then begged for news about Robert. "Mr. West is still in critical condition, Ms. Brooks, but his vital signs are improving. He was in shock when he arrived and it has been touch and go, as you

Americans say, but I am more inclined to say that he will live after today's examination."

"When can I see him?" she asked.

"You will be allowed to sit in a chair today; perhaps tomorrow you could be wheeled to our intensive care unit for a very brief visit. You must go slowly, Ms. Brooks, your own injuries will take time to heal," he said. Just then a man entered the room. He spoke to the doctor in almost a whisper. The doctor nodded his head to signal his agreement. "Ms. Brooks, this is Lt. Alejandro Alhambra from our city police, he would like to ask you a few questions. I will see you tomorrow." The surgeon turned and left the room and the police detective walked closer to Penny's bed. He spoke broken English, asking Penny to explain the circumstances of the shooting. She began with the attempts on the lives of her grandparents, after the sighting of a war criminal, the death of Anthony West and then the author, Robert Wellington and the planned trip to Germany to see the scientist, Artur Goldberg and the faxes he had sent; then the monk at their hotel door, who shot them both. The detective seemed to take a couple of minutes to digest all that Penny had said. She grew impatient and broke into his thoughts, "Can you tell me if the documents were found in our hotel room?" she asked, "they are very important."

"I will have to check with our property department," Ms. Brooks,

"I do not recall everything that was taken from the scene of the shooting. If they were in the hotel room then they should be logged into the property room. Once we released the hotel room, everything was removed at the request of the hotel. You will be given another room should you choose to return to the hotel." He paused, still thinking, it seemed, about all that Penny had told him.

"Do you think this man was a real monk?" Ms Brooks.

"I have no way of knowing that for sure, but I would say he was. It was his demeanor even with a gun in his hand. The lieutenant could not begin to imagine a monk doing such a thing nor how he would begin to find him. He should probably start with the airport to see if a monk had arrived or left *Malaga* in the past 48 hours and where he went.

"Thank you for speaking with me," he said, "I wish both you and Mr. West a speedy recovery. I will let you know, as soon as practical, about the documents." He turned and left the room.

Penny decided that she had better call her grandparents. At her request, no one from the hospital or the police were to contact them. It was a difficult call because she knew it would be terribly upsetting for both her grandparents. Another shooting. Would it never end? After talking to both, they were convinced that she was going to be alright, but were deeply concerned about Robert. Her grandfather would call the Manhattan D.A.'s office to inform them of the shooting and the seriousness of Robert's condition.

Two days later a representative of the NYC prosecutor's office stood at Penny's bedside. It was Timothy Witten, the man who spoke to Robert when they were having lunch at the Waldorf. He looked to be Robert's age of thirty-two. He wanted to know if there was anything he could do for Robert or herself. Since the lieutenant had not yet contacted her regarding the documents, perhaps Timothy would be a good person (a representative of the NYC prosecutor's office) to intervene with the lieutenant. Should she have Timothy take them back to the prosecutor's office? She really wanted to make another copy before giving them to anyone. She planned to do that at the hotel, but the shooter interrupted that plan. For some reason she decided to wait. Perhaps she could get someone from the hospital to scan and e-mail copies to her own e-mail address. She did not know this man well enough to entrust him with the only copy of these documents.

"I really can't think of a thing," Mr. Witten, "but thank you for the offer."

"I have already spoken to the police and have a copy of their incident report that my supervisor wanted me to get. I'll probably stay another day. Robert was barely able to speak when I saw him earlier. Maybe by tomorrow he'll be able to carry on a conversation. Then I must return, I have a case going to trial in a few days and need to finish my preparations," he finished.

"It was nice of you to come all this distance. It sounds as if we are both on the mend, but it will be a while before Robert is well enough to travel. We will just have to take things one day at a time. I'm sure Robert will contact your office when he is able," she said.

Timothy returned to New York City and Penny was discharged from the hospital three days later. The police detective brought the suitcases with him that had been stored in the property room and drove Penny to a different hotel to register. He insisted that she register under a different name and stayed until she was ensconced in her room. It was actually a suite with two bedrooms and a sitting room with a complete entertainment system and, also, a wet bar. Her grandfather had prepaid the hotel for a month's stay, she was told. The lieutenant also turned over the documents that were found in the hotel room. They all appeared intact and Penny wondered why the monk didn't steal the documents. Perhaps he was frightened-off by another hotel guest? She visited with Robert, just before she left the hospital, and was somewhat relieved to see that he was doing much better. He had been moved from the intensive care unit to the surgical care floor. He would probably have to remain at the hospital for another ten days to two weeks.

Penny stayed in the hotel room and ordered room service for all her meals. She was very weak, but as the days went by her strength gradually returned. She was awkward with one arm strapped to her body, but she took a cab to the hospital each day and spent two hours in the morning and two hours in the evening with Robert and returned to the hotel. She was lonely without him. Her heart ached to see how much pain he was still having.

It was another three weeks before Robert was released from the hospital with the understanding that it would be another two weeks before he could even think about traveling. He had a lot of internal healing to do and could not do anything to tear apart the internal stitches. He was a good patient and began to get back his appetite. They still ate their meals in their room and while they held hands and kissed, they were not able to make love because of both of their conditions.

The days passed quickly in spite of their limitations and by the tenth day after his discharge, Penny's collarbone restrictive bandage was removed and Robert felt strong enough to take a taxi so they could eat somewhere besides the hotel; they were getting bored by the menu. The evening went well and when they returned to the hotel Robert said, "Penny, I want to marry you. Let's not wait. Let's find out how we can have a civil ceremony here and when we get home, we can

do it in a church, if you want. What do you say?"

"Robert, I'll marry you anywhere, anytime. I love you with all my heart and soul." Three days later they were married in a simple ceremony. That night, for the first time in over a month they made love, although some of their passion had to be harnessed so that no one would get hurt. Penny called and told her grandparents who insisted on a church ceremony at home. Penny agreed, but made clear to them that in the eyes of the law, they were married. They returned home ten days later with tans that were the envy of their friends.

Chapter Eleven

Lake George, New York
November 3, 2005

The Adirondack Mountains, in the fall, are a sight to behold and fortunately there was an extended fall season and some of the leaves still maintained their color even so late in the season. They had changed to red, orange and some, a magnificent purple. Penny had decided that they would drive from the city to the lake, to take the time to enjoy the scenery. Penny enjoyed driving and Robert said he would be able to spell her when she grew tired. Most of the soreness in his abdomen had receded and he was beginning to feel his own self, again, but neither could forget, for a moment, how close to death they had come - especially Robert.

They were both determined to more completely understand the Goldberg documents and thought Laurence might help them or knew who they might see to help them. Robert was treated as the return of the prodigal son. Both Laurence and Giselle knew that Robert had nearly died, as his father did, trying to help them. They were pleased by the marriage, but wanted to "do it up properly," as her grandfather explained. They were to decide where and when and then Penny's grandparents would do the rest. It would be "their show."

Laurence took the documents to his study and did not appear, again, for nearly three hours. "This is really something," he said in almost a whisper. If Krueger has something like this, why haven't we heard anything from him for all of these years? I understand the Vatican blackmail, but he could do more - cause all kinds of chaos with this thing. Why hasn't he? He's an old man, now; his time is running out. It's almost too late for him, isn't it?" Robert was pensive and then the proverbial light bulb lit.

"Because he is turning it over to a son or a daughter to continue the blackmail of the Vatican. Maybe that's all he wants, now; maybe he'd rather have continuing wealth for his family than to become a world leader like Hitler. Maybe he just didn't have the stomach for politics or the resurrection of the Nazi party. He wants to be more respectable. I'll bet he lives here, in the US, and is a wealthy man. Penny and I really need to get to the records at Ellis Island and try to identify this man. He is going to be a continuing threat to all of us and I don't intend to live my life looking over my shoulder!" Robert exclaimed.

Penny and Robert had missed Octoberfest that both grandparents loved to attend. Laurence liked his beer and everyone loves an 'oompah band.' Penny told Robert about the times she had spent with her grandparents at the festival - where they ate sausage and sauerkraut as they enjoyed watching the polka dancers in native costumes. Dessert was usually *apfelstruddel* and coffee. Penny loved anything European, especially the people and food. Her grandfather told her that his mother was German and, with a French grandmother, she *was* European!

They stayed for a couple of days, but Penny was anxious to get back to the city - they had a lot of work to do to uncover the identity of Krueger.

Chapter Twelve

New York City
November 5, 2005

Penny wanted to get to the records at Ellis Island and she thought Robert should rest in the afternoon; he was still recovering his strength. Robert was staying at Penny's condo. They had not yet decided whether they would keep Robert's inherited brownstone or live in the condo. They both had such busy lives that the condo had a lot of attraction, especially located right on 5th Avenue in the heart of Manhattan. Penny spent all day at Ellis Island and called Robert about five o'clock and said she was on her way home; she suggested that they go to Gallagher's for steak. When Penny reached thirty she started receiving five-thousand dollars a month from her trust fund. With the condo owned outright, she did not have to hurry back to work at the newspaper. Although her boss had left several messages on her answering machine, she had not yet called him. She would do that tomorrow, but she wasn't going back until they found out Krueger's new identity. Her boss would have to wait and if he couldn't, she was sure she would have no difficulty starting at another paper when she was ready. (Thank you, Daddy, for the freedom your foresight has given me, she thought.)

Penny had made it through three month's of names in the year of 1943. They had started that far back in case Krueger left close to the time he been ordered back to *Berchtesgaden* from France and his encounter with Giselle. She had photocopied the logs at Ellis Island and as they sat down to dinner, Penny handed half to Robert. "This is going to be a working dinner," she smiled, "do you see any names that strike you, or perhaps an age that seems the most likely?"

"If your grandfather is right, this guy is his age; so, at war's end, he would have been twenty-six or twenty-seven; why don't we concentrate on the age?" Penny had been turning pages, rather quickly, and suddenly stopped and looked deep in thought.

"What is it Penny? Have you found something?"

"Didn't you tell me that Timothy is the son of the senator, Karl Witten?"

"Yes."

"Well, his grandfather entered from England by way of Switzerland and it states that he is a banker," Penny said. "That would be a great cover, wouldn't it? Coming to open a branch bank in New York City?"

"Timothy's grandfather is a well-known banker; well known on

Wall Street, at least. Also a very wealthy man. When did he come?" Robert asked.

"February 25, 1943. Just about a month after Krueger's visit to the Vatican Bank. It's him! I just know it! He is a wealthy man according to you and has a son running for the White House! It's just the perfect scenario, isn't it? Give the manuscript to a new president and he could do much more than blackmail the Vatican, couldn't he?" she questioned.

"You're right. It all fits. We need to get a photograph; see if your grandparents can identify Witten as Krueger. You operate your own camera, don't you? Do you have a telephoto lens?" he asked. "Let's find out where he lives and then we'll try to get a decent photo, don't you agree?"

"It sounds like a plan to me, and I have a digital camera with a telephoto lens," replied Penny.

They found Witten's address from the phone book and the next morning they headed to Riverside Drive to park across the street from Witten's building. Penny had made some ham and cheese sandwiches and a large thermos of coffee. It was mid-afternoon before he came out of the building and Penny took a lot of digital photos. They rushed back to their condo so they could upload the digital images to Penny's computer. She spent nearly a half-hour editing the images and announced she was finished. They were great photos; she called her grandfather to tell him to start his computer, she was sending him pictures that might be Karl Krueger.

About 30 minutes later her grandfather called on the telephone and said, "It's him! How did you find him? Where is he living? What's his new identity?"

"It was surprisingly easy, *Grandpere*. We started with the Ellis Island logs and luckily picked the right year to start our search. We already had a profile in mind. Everything fit. He is Karl Witten, a bank owner," she replied.

"Is the senator his son? My God! He could be the next president! No wonder Giselle always thought the senator looked vaguely familiar! Now that I think about it, there is a resemblance. The senator's features are softer. His eyes are blue, but without the coldness of his father's," he seemed to wind down.

Robert piped-up, "That's why the father was at Lake George. His son announced his candidacy at the hotel up there!"

"Did you hear that, *Grandpere*?" asked Penny.

"Of course, that must be why we are a danger to him; his plan for his son's future. He's probably going to finance the bid for the White House with the fortune he obtained through the blackmail of the Vatican. We have got to expose him!" replied her grandfather. Robert had already grabbed another extension of the phone in the kitchen, "We will expose him, Laurence, but we need to learn a little more about this manuscript. Did you come-up with any names of the kind of scientist we need to verify Goldberg's findings?"

"Yes. There is a physicist at Columbia who has agreed to meet with you. If someone from another scientific discipline is needed he will contact that person. His name is David MacIntyre and you can reach him at 212-555-7820. He's a nice fellow and as bright as they come. He should be able to determine whether those drawings, charts and diagrams mean what Goldberg says they mean. Call me after you have talked to him. I can't wait until we can get rid of these armed guards and live a normal life, once again. How are you feeling, Robert?" he asked.

"I am doing well, Laurence, almost back to my old self," Robert replied.

"What's the 'almost'?," asked Laurence.

"Oh, nothing much. I just tire faster than I used to," replied Robert.

"You've been through a lot, young man. You almost died! Pace yourself. I'll let you go, but please call me after you have met with Mac Intyre." He hung-up the phone.

Chapter Thirteen

Columbia University
November 7, 2005

David MacIntrye looked to be a man in his early forties; tall, with sandy hair and brown eyes. He had a ready smile and judging by the neatness of his desk, was not the typical absent-minded professor. Penny explained the provenance of the documents they carried and asked if he would look at them and tell them what he thought they were.

"Did you say these documents came from Artur Goldberg?" he asked. "I have known Artur for many years and have a deep respect for his theoretical work."

"Yes. He thought it too dangerous to meet in Germany, so he faxed these documents to us," Robert said.

"I understand. Penny's grandfather explained all about the violence of the past few months and that these documents may be behind these actions. May I see them?" he asked. Penny handed the documents to MacIntyre and he sat down at his desk, while Penny and Robert took the two chairs opposite the desk. Dr. MacIntyre was totally engrossed in the copies of Goldberg's notes. It appeared he was just glancing at each page from the way he kept flipping through the twenty pages, but he returned to a couple of the pages and then looked up at Penny and Robert.

"This is possible," he spoke, "it would never have occurred to me that that was the true meaning, but I can see it, now. This is very exciting! I can see why the Vatican might yield to blackmail. The drawings of the device are especially intriguing. May I call in a colleague to look at them?" he asked. Penny had not wanted to leave copies to be passed around to a lot of people, so she was pleasantly surprised when MacIntyre picked up the telephone and called his colleague, who arrived about ten minutes later.

Without any preamble, Dr. MacIntyre handed the drawing to his colleague and said, "John, just look at this and tell me what you think it is." John took the document and studied it for about five minutes and said, "This is a type of laser that would be used for long distance telecommunications. It is more advanced than anything we have produced yet; the attached plates look like something used in electrophoresis or maybe an advanced electron microscope. Whose design is this?" he asked.

""We're not sure, John. Thanks for taking the time to come up. When we solve the mystery of ownership, I'll let you know," said Mac Intyre. When John left the room, MacIntyre returned to his desk and spoke. "I think I have it," he said, "that's a laser-operated computer that is used to analyze blood and tissue samples, like an electronic microscope, and those results are sent somewhere through laser communication. That is the purpose of the semi-precious gem in the overall design. I think Goldberg is right that it is a sapphire with a titanium chip. It blows my mind that that is exactly what Jewish legend states it was thousands of years ago, and that information, in the right hands, would have entirely changed the perception of events in some biblical stories; this changes everything we have believed about the more recent past (on the whole yardstick of time), doesn't it? I am reviewing a lot of things in my head that, now, may have an entirely new meaning. This is so exciting! May I keep this set of copies?" he asked.

"Once we have published what this find is really all about," you may have a set of copies, Doctor," spoke Robert, "we need to keep this quiet until we can publish. You do understand that we may have placed you in danger just by coming to your office? There can be no safety for us all until this is no longer a secret from the world. If everyone knows what's in these documents, there can be no blackmail; no reason to shoot people," he finished.

"I do understand, Mr. West; I accepted the risk to, hopefully, solve the mystery that is causing so much bloodshed. It is a powerful tool you hold in your hands. The truth about its origin can be used for good or evil. In any event, it will shake-up the world and after the chaos, there will be a new enlightenment, a new truth. If I can be of any further assistance, please call. I will watch for the publication of what you have found, with great interest," MacIntyre said as he stood. Robert and Penny stood, shook hands with the famous scientist and headed back to the condo to digest everything. Both Robert and Penny were lost in their own thoughts on the drive back to their condo. Penny spoke first, "Robert, do you understand the significance of this? According to Artur Goldberg, that is a drawing of an actual device, purported to be thousands of years old, but is more advanced than our present computers and lasers. How is that possible? How could one of the Knights Templar be in possession of such a device? Do you believe that Goldberg is right? That it is the Ark of the Covenant and Hitler found it or it was given to him?"

"I don't see how we can doubt Goldberg; it was given to Hitler by Ante Pavelic where it was found hidden in a mine where it had been since the days of the Knights Templar. I did a little research while you spent the day at Ellis Island and discovered that the Knights Templar were concentrated in France and were either killed or disbursed by Philip the Fair in October 1307. Those that survived the order of death escaped to other countries. It seems entirely possible that one may have escaped to *Yugoslavia* or what is now *Croatia*. Pavelic traded the device with Hitler for autonomy over *Croatia* during the war. Pavelic wanted his own little empire. It was a Franciscan monk who told Pavelic what the device is. He did all the measurements and proved to Pavelic that it conformed to ancient descriptions of the device. Hitler had an inordinate interest in finding religious objects; he wanted to end the power of the Vatican, or, as it turned out, to bend the papacy to his will," Robert finished.

"This is going to be upsetting for millions, if not billions of worshipers of both the Judeo and Christian faiths. It is going to turn the Christian church inside-out isn't it? Do you think they (the popes and Vatican government) have known, all along, what the Ark really is?" Penny asked.

"There is no doubt the papacy has known since the war, but if you go back to ancient biblical times, the Ark was in the possession of the ancient Jewish priesthood and was lost during the second destruction of the Temple of Solomon. It was the ancient Jewish priesthood that covered up its loss. We have to rethink everything we have been taught about these ancient times," said Robert.

"I wish we could have a long conversation with Goldberg," mused Penny, "I would like to know what he has concluded about how this device came into existence."

"Speaking of Goldberg, how are we going to keep his name out of your newspaper article? He is an essential part of the story, how can he remain nameless?" asked Robert.

"I've been thinking about him, myself. I wonder if he would agree to come to America, until all this business is over; I can't bear the thought of putting his life in jeopardy, but I need his imprimatur on his own notes. We can't tell the story without him," Penny said, "is there any way we can take him into protective custody?"

"That's a thought," mused Robert, "let me think about that." Just as Robert finished his last thought, his car was hit from behind. Robert looked in his rearview mirror and saw one of those new cars that look like a tank. The car backed off and Robert thought it was an old man driver who misjudged his speed - an accident. He was proven wrong when he was hit so hard, again, that he was forced to hit a parked car on the street. The tank whizzed by as Robert opened his door, but he managed to get three letters and two numbers of the license plate. He called the police on his cell phone and they arrived just five minutes later. He identified himself as an ADA (Assistance District Attorney), explained what happened and gave the abbreviated license number to the police, but he knew who was driving that tank; it was Witten, the elder. It was a foolish thing to attempt in the city; there would not be enough speed to injure anyone seriously, but maybe that wasn't the point. Maybe it was just Witten's way of telling them that he knew they had been watching him, photographing him. A not-so-subtle warning. The right fender of the car was caved-in, so it was towed to a garage for the insurance adjuster to appraise and the body shop to repair; in the meantime they would use Penny's BMW. Robert was upset about the car; it was his father's. Robert did not own a car before his father was killed; he took the bus or a taxi to and from work. He had arranged for an additional parking spot in the parking garage where Penny housed her car. He thought the second car might be needed during their investigation. It pained him to see the damage; it was just a way to hang-on to his father a little longer.

Robert had decided that it was time to have a face-to-face with his boss, Jonathan Mc Carthy, about all that had been happening and the deeper reason for it. He made an appointment for the following morning and Penny would accompany him. They would lay out the whole thing: the Nazi war criminal, the Vatican blackmail, the senator-son, the attack at *Costa del Sol* and the manuscript that was based on Goldberg's notes, and Dr. MacIntyre's opinion.

Penny and Robert had taken turns, talking for almost an hour before they had covered all the material. The district attorney was lost in thought for several minutes after he viewed Goldberg's notes. "I agree that we need to protect Goldberg and you do need his gravitas to make this story credible. We can arrest Witten and keep him behind bars until extradition to Germany, but I owe the senator a heads-up. I know him quite well and his son, Timothy, has been with this office for three years. That should take the teeth out of this violence; you both are very lucky to be alive. Who would have believed that Karl Witten Sr. is a war criminal? He, and his bank, have become as much a part of Wall Street as the big board. He has amassed a fortune and I guess the Vatican provided the seed money, huh?"

"I think it was more than seed money," replied Robert. Ten crates filled with paintings, *objects d'art* and jewelry stolen from the Jews would be worth a fortune in today's dollars. I'll bet this stuff was liquidated so that Witten could buy his bank. When was that, I have forgotten?"

Penny replied, "I think that was in the mid-sixties, I have got the date at home. Mr. McCarthy, my grandparents will have to be a part of any trial, won't they? Since they have identified Witten's picture?"

"Yes, they will. I think they should come to NYC as soon as possible to give a deposition, so that we can arrest this son-of-a-bitch. I will call the senator to see if he will surrender his father. This may destroy his bid for the White House and will be personally devastating; I doubt he knows anything about his father's background. Well, Ms Brooks, I can arrange a flight for your grandparents, if that's agreeable," finished the district attorney.

"Neither of my grandparents is able to deal with the hassle of flying, anymore. If it is alright with you, I will arrange for a limo to bring them to the Rensselaer train station, which they would much prefer, and I will meet the train, here. At their ages, they will need to rest a while before their official identification of Krueger. If I get them here tomorrow, could this take place the following day?" Penny asked.

"That will be fine, Ms. Brooks," he replied.

Laurence and Giselle Penrose-Brooks arrived the following day at 3PM. Penny was at Grand Central Station in plenty of time to meet their train and she wasn't the only one waiting for the couple to arrive. As they walked the concourse to the 42nd street exit, shots rang out. Penny rushed her grandparents inside a bakery on the same concourse and stuck her head above the display case to see where the shooter was. Her head came close to being blown off; she ducked just in time. She grabbed her cell phone and called 911. They were trapped. Each time she made the slightest move, a bullet whizzed by. She thought the shooter was located at a newspaper kiosk about fifty feet away. She got a glimpse of a man who appeared to be in his forties, with dark hair and eyes. He wasn't shooting randomly; this was an attempt to prevent her grandparents from making an official identification and giving a deposition. She had asked the 911 operator to contact the district attorney's office and tell him what was happening. She did not have time to call Robert. It was ten minutes of pure fear before she heard sirens coming closer and about ten police officers, in uniform, were running down the stairs into the concourse. The shooting had stopped; the shooter heard the sirens and disappeared. Penny was trying to explain the details of what was happening, but it wasn't until the district attorney appeared that they truly understood that this was a deliberate act and not some nut who had gone off his rocker.

"How could they have known my grandparents were arriving, today?" asked Penny of the district attorney. "Neither Robert or I told a soul. I don't understand!"

"I am afraid I do, Ms Brooks. This is my fault and I am terribly sorry. I called the senator to encourage him to surrender his father without a lot of fanfare. I explained that the official identification would take place tomorrow. He must have known that it would be your grandparents making the ID and hired a gun to stakeout the station. The senator must know that his father *is* Krueger and about the manuscript. With your grandparents dead there could be no arrest. I am truly sorry, Mr. and Mrs. Penrose-Brooks. From this moment forward you will be under the protection of the district attorney's office. We will arrange for accommodations for you and your wife, as well as Robert and Penny until this arrest is made. You will not be able to stay in your condo, Ms Brooks; I am sure they know where you live," said the district attorney.

"I had better call Robert and have him pack a few clothes. Where should he meet us?" Penny asked. "Tell him to come to the office; we need to make some plans. I want Krueger arrested, now! I'll need to get a warrant and will need your grandparents to do the deposition, now. I know you all are probably exhausted, but we need to move up our timetable. There will either be another attempt to kill you both or Krueger will run knowing that he has exhausted all his opportunities to kill you. I need to put out alerts for the airports, and a general all-points bulletin for his car. We can't lose him, now; we are so close to ending this nightmare for all of you," he said.

Laurence nodded his head in agreement and turned to Giselle. "Can you manage, Luv? Just a few more hours and it will be over?"

"I will do whatever I have to do to see this monster brought to justice, but I need to sit somewhere where it is quiet. Maybe a nice cup of tea? Can you arrange that Mr. McCarthy?" Giselle asked.

"We have a nice lounge at our office. Most people will be gone, it's five o'clock, so it should be quiet. Let's get out of this place," he replied. He ushered Laurence, Giselle and Penny to a waiting limousine. There was a police car in front and one in back of the limo as they made their way to the district attorney's office. They made it there without incident. Giselle and Laurence were shown to the lounge where they could rest while the DA prepared the arrest warrant for Krueger. He gave it to an assistant to get a judge's signature, then the police would be sent to arrest Karl Witten Sr. a/k/a Karl Krueger. Giselle and Laurence had just finished giving their deposition, when the cops returned without Karl Kreuger. There was no answer at their condo. The conclusion was that they had skipped-out after the last failure to kill the Penrose-Brooks couple. Everyone was deflated; they thought it would be over that evening.

The DA decided to call the senator; this time he would not try to spare the man any embarrassment, "Mr. Witten, if you do not produce your father, this evening, your political career will be over."

"You seem to think that I am my father's keeper. I informed him that he would be arrested, as you requested, and asked him to tell me when he would be ready to surrender and I would accompany him. I have not been able to reach him, by telephone, all day. I know nothing more about his or my mother's whereabouts. What more can I say or do?" he asked.

"You should be made aware, if you are not already, that there was another attempt on the people who have identified your father as Karl Krueger. Only you or your father could have arranged for a shooter to be at Grand Central Station waiting for them," replied the district attorney.

"I beg your pardon; I would not be party to such a thing! How could I possibly know where or when to place such a person and where would I find such a person - to commit murder? You are barking up the wrong tree, Mr. McCarthy. I suggest you do what you have to do with regard to my father, but I am not a party to any attempts to thwart the law! Good day!" he said as his slammed the phone down.

The DA was mulling over what the senator had to say. He had acquitted himself quite well and how could he know that the Penrose-Brooks' were coming by train that day? Could it just be an educated guess? Witten and his wife were, also, in their eighties; would they really try to make a run for it at their ages? It just didn't seem likely. Maybe a search warrant for their home would turn up some clues as to their whereabouts? He sent his assistant, again, to interrupt a judge's dinner. An hour later they were entering the Witten's condo. Penny and Robert, the DA and four police officers started walking through the kitchen, dining room and living room. It was a beautiful condo, with expensive furniture and wall coverings; it was the epitome of the good life that Krueger had provided his wife and family.

There was a shout from another part of the condo and everyone ran to see what was wrong. They entered a large bedroom and found Karl Krueger and his wife - dead in each other's arms; an apparent double suicide. Everyone was told not to touch a thing while the DA called the medical examiner and crime scene investigators. Robert and Penny were deflated that they couldn't bring this man to justice, but at the same time were relieved for Penny's grandparents. They would be asked to make an ID, but then it was over for them. They could go back to Lake George and live out their days in peace.

A week later, after returning to Lake George with her grandparents, seeing them settled, Penny returned to work. She had the go-ahead from her editor to write the story of Karl Krueger, the Nazi hiding under their noses as a successful banker, but he wanted her to hold-off writing anything about the nature of the Krueger manuscript. Penny argued, until she was red-in-the-face, that the public had a right to know what was in the manuscript. Her editor refused. Penny quit. After long discussions with Robert, Penny decided to write a book about the whole story. They could live very comfortably on Robert's salary and her trust fund; she didn't have to work at a newspaper, at all.

The newspapers covered the deaths of Witten and his wife, but did not reveal that he was a Nazi war criminal. Penny saw the powerful

influence of the senator at work; obviously he intended to pursue his candidacy for president and was able to convince the owners of the newspapers that what his father did, or did not do, during the war had nothing to do with him. Publishing that information would be highly prejudicial. Penny could hear it all; imagine it all, but she intended that her book be published before the election in 2008. The senator could be the one now blackmailing the Vatican or whomever. What about the manuscript? Did the senator have it? Was it with his father's possessions? In a safe deposit box? At his bank?

Chapter Fourteen

Robert and Timothy Witten often went for a drink after work; Penny thought it strange, after all that had happened, that they should become drinking buddies. Timothy said he was shocked to learn that his grandfather was a Nazi war criminal, but he loved him anyway and that was about the extent of that particular conversation. He was excited that his father was doing so well in the political campaign; the television polls had him leading by four points. Penny wondered what his poll numbers would be if they knew how right wing he really was and the truth was known about his father's past and the fact that there is a manuscript, still out there, that was used to successfully blackmail the Vatican. She thought it was high-time that the truth be told.

She had met with MacIntyre and the man who had identified one of the drawings as a laser, John Engle, and got their opinions and permission for publication. The only thing remaining was the trip to Germany and to incorporate any new material into the book. Robert would not let Penny travel alone. He took three days off (no trials pending) and they left for Munich on *Lufthansa*. They arrived late in the day and called to confirm their meeting for the next morning. If Penny got what she wanted from Goldberg, they might take the night flight back to New York City.

Munich, Germany

Goldberg looked to be a man of at least one-hundred years old. He was hunched-over, walked with the assistance of a walker, but his mind was clear as a bell. He took Penny and Robert into his office that looked like it had been struck by a hurricane. Despite his age, Goldberg still dabbled in theoretical physics and still wrote articles for science journals. His wife had died and his children lived away; one in *Bonn*, the other in *Hof*. He was very much alone with his thoughts. His housekeeper came in every day to clean (although allowed in the office only once in a blue moon) and to shop for groceries and prepare his dinner. He seemed happy to have some visitors. There was a fresh pot of coffee on a hotplate which he offered to his guests. Penny got up and poured for all of them.

"Dr. Goldberg, as I told you, I am writing a book about Krueger and the manuscript. You know what David MacIntyre and John Engle told me about the drawings. I need your *gravitas* to publish a book

that is truly going to awaken the world. Are you willing to reveal what you did for Hitler, for publication?" she asked.

"I am an old man and never one to be afraid of being called names, but Ms Brooks, are you ready for what will come once you publish this information? You could be branded a crackpot, no matter what science brings to the table. People will not readily accept this information. Some will become very angry. You will be shaking the very foundation of many, many lives," he replied.

"If we have been all wrong in our interpretation of biblical literature, don't you think that wrong should be corrected? Don't you think the majority of the population would want to know the truth?" she queried.

"I do not know about majority," he said, "but I am a scientist and a Jew and I found it upsetting on both levels; as a scientist, it challenges science's retrieval of human history and as a practicing Jew, I confess that it requires a whole new interpretation of the Pentateuch, the foundation of our Jewish beliefs. I do not doubt, for a moment, that what we found is true, but it still is upsetting. To have seen the past with a lens that is so out of focus is upsetting, but you must understand that this new understanding is only possible because of the advances that we have made through science and technology. We would not have had the framework to understand the purpose of the device

without our march to a more civilized and technological society. We could not understand what was found even one hundred years ago. Do you understand what I am saying, Ms Brooks?" he asked.

"Yes, that is clear to me; but we will always have a distorted view if we do not correct that flawed lens. Don't you think modern societies have progressed enough to 'receive' this information? Perhaps not sixty years ago, when you found the device, but certainly now," she replied. "We have sent people to the moon and probes to the far solar system; we are cloning sheep and are using bio-technology to ease human suffering."

"Perhaps you are right, Ms Brooks, let us hope so. If the charts have been correctly interpreted, we are going to be forced to face this truth within a few years anyway. Perhaps your book will serve society well as a preparation for what is to come," Dr. Goldberg said.

"Even the Vatican has its own observatory and has intensified its quest for cosmic truths; its new observatory at Tucson, Arizona and the Jesuits' lead in these pursuits makes me wonder if they do not have a knowledge of what *is* to come;" said Robert, "why are they not preparing their Christian flock?

"I do not know their reasons," said Goldberg. "Their interest in scientific knowledge has certainly intensified since the war; perhaps it has always been more than their publicly stated purpose of building a

bridge between faith and science. They no longer have to study the skies to determine the accuracy of the calendar. I guess they no longer believe that the world was created a mere six thousand years ago, but much of what they are studying, now, has nothing to do with their mandate; they are seeking scientific knowledge as aggressively as many other observatories around the world and they are watching and waiting. One can only wonder if the manuscript intensified their search of the heavens."

"Dr. Goldberg, do you know everything that was in the original manuscript? Did you see the finished product?" asked Robert.

"Oh, yes; I was project manager. Each of the scientists was required to read his section for any possible errors. Hitler was a real stickler in all things, but even the project manager was under intense SS supervision. It is probably the most important document ever assembled. If Hitler had been successful in his quest to rule the nations of the world, he would have dismantled all religious institutions and named himself the King of the Earth. Thank God for the Allies!" he said.

"Can you confirm a few details for me, Dr. Goldberg?" asked Penny.

"Certainly," he replied.

"There is no doubt in your mind that what is described in the manuscript is the Ark of the Covenant?" she asked.

"None, whatsoever. The measurements conform to the biblical descriptions. To understand what it really is, one must shut out the vision of your Mr. Heston, as Moses, carrying down the stone tablets from the mount. The real tablets conform more to the Jewish legends that they were really sapphires. It has only been since the 80's that the sapphire with a titanium chip was developed in lasers to be used for long distance telecommunications. It is absolutely clear to every scientist involved in the project that this was a major purpose of the Ark of the Covenant and the original tabernacle was, as you know, a portable tent to protect this device from the desert sands. The first house of worship, on this earth, was not a place for people to come and say prayers to an omnipresent god; it was a place to house a remarkable scientific device that allowed the ancient priesthood to communicate scientific information to a distant and specific place," he paused.

"My next question is - what scientific information do you think was being conveyed?" asked Penny.

"We have totally misunderstood the sacrifice of animals in the early tabernacle; it was not for the purpose generally believed - the shedding of animal blood just to appease a powerful God. In retrospect, it is now clear that the practices described in the Pentateuch and the development of later Jewish practices is that these animals were being tested for disease and even for the fat and nutritional content. The Jewish dietary laws that survive today are the by-product of this early testing. The *High Priest* of this portable temple was the only one who communicated with Yahweh - from the place on the Ark that was called the *Place of Mercy* and he was, obviously, a senior technician. This is the place where we found a microphone and speaker. If you just forget that this device is over five thousand years old, it is pretty simple to understand within today's technology," stated Dr. Goldberg. "Even sixty years ago, it was a great challenge for all the German scientists assembled by Hitler. It took nine months of round-the-clock research and analysis to duplicate the components of this device, what we call 'reverse-engineering,' and to make it work. When it was finally tested in the fall of 1942, Hitler's belief that it would communicate with extraterrestrial intelligent beings (perhaps even those that created us) was vindicated. While many believe that the modern UFO era began with the sightings by an American in 1947, that era actually began five years earlier with the very first sighting of a spaceship over Turin on November 28, 1942, just three months after the device was first activated. But, even before the ship was sighted, there was a strange phenomenon that began to occur in September of 1942 that came to be called "foo fighters." These strange balls of light followed German, American and British aircraft. It is my belief that these were some kind of probes sent to analyze our aircraft. In any case, the device seemed to open the door to extraterrestrial visitation."

Penny was about to ask another question, but the professor said in an afterthought, "It is worth mentioning that after the destruction of the first permanent temple, the Temple of Solomon," animal sacrifice was abandoned, but was started, again, after the temple was rebuilt. It is clear that until the Ark was recovered from the rubble and operating again there was no purpose to the sacrifice of animals. This is an actual historical confirmation of its real purpose. Of course, it was eventually lost around 800 B.C. Do you understand the significance of losing this device? Everything since then, in Temple and later Christian churches has just become an empty ritual. It can truly be called the greatest tragedy and cover-up in human history; we, literally, lost contact with a creator who intended to monitor our food supply, physical development and our general health!" he finally finished.

"Dr. Goldberg, that leads me to probably the most important question; where were these communications going? We know to whom, but where?" asked Penny.

"We would have had no idea, whatsoever, without the charts that were included in the memory chip. These signals were being sent to an unknown planet in our own solar system, possibly bounced off a satellite they placed in orbit around Earth, Mars or some near location. The chart demonstrates that this planet has a huge eccentricity of orbit that takes it far beyond Pluto to nearer the Oort Cloud and back to within a few million miles of Jupiter. In other words, Jupiter can be said to be the sun of this planet, not the sun around which all the other planets orbit. While there is no attempt in the chart to show any numbers, all the scientists on this project agreed the orbit would take 5,124 years to complete, and incidentally, this is the exact number of years in the Mayan calendar. They have, apparently, retained an ancient memory of the last time this planet entered our solar system near Jupiter. The Mayan calendar begins at 3,113 BC and ends at 2,012 AD which is when we all agreed this planet would become visible to our telescopes. Another point worth mentioning is that the BC date is the time that most agree the Great Pyramid at Giza was built."

"Can a signal really travel that far, Dr. Goldberg?" asked Robert.

"Oh yes, indeed. A laser signal would be traveling at the speed of light or about 6 trillion miles per year; that is well beyond our furthest planet - Pluto," he replied, which is only .0008 of a light year distant from the sun, at its maximum orbital distance," he replied. "As very strange as all of this may sound, it is all very possible from a scientific point of view. There are those who have had to consider how any human-like race could survive without the sunlight we require, but a far advanced race of beings such as described in the early BIBLE would probably have solved that problem by creating artificial sunlight and probably MUCH further advanced than our light bulbs, *Ja*? We must not impose our own limitations on a society that was clearly already versed in bio-engineering (which is how we were created) and probably had already harnessed nuclear energy," he finished.

"Do you think the Star of Bethlehem was this planet, Dr. Goldberg?" asked Robert.

"No, I think the Star of Bethlehem was a spaceship *from* this planet. A star would not follow people as they traveled throughout the ancient lands as described in the BIBLE, but a spaceship would, and a large one would appear very much like a moving star," he replied.

"I understand the Ark of the Covenant as you have explained it, professor, and even an undiscovered planet, but what about Jesus? How does He fit into this story?" asked Penny.

"Let's just review the broad strokes of what has been recorded in biblical literature and how it works with what has been revealed by reverse-engineering the Ark, shall we?" he asked. "Someone - an individual who the ancient Jews called Yahweh - created the universe and our solar system and the first human being on earth. He created Adam and then took one of his ribs and created Eve. No self-respecting scientist could accept that a female version of Yahweh's creation (Eve) could be created from a rib; but, if you take that word as a metonymic symbol, it works perfectly. Something was taken from Adam's body, something that denotes *structure* (as a bone would) and something that Adam could live without, it becomes a perfect word for the modern equivalent - 'gene.' Rib was a perfectly appropriate word for a young, superstitious society in awe of the beings who created them and demonstrated skills far beyond their comprehension, but could be better understood by an adult society. This 'thing' was used to create a female version of Adam and with just a little genetic modification, actually little was required of a genetic engineer to accomplish this. Remember, Yahweh said, 'Let *us* make man in our image.' Who was he talking to? He wasn't alone, he was the boss, the mission commander and/or the king of this unknown planet. To his creations, Yahweh was truly a god, a title often given to forces that could not be understood, (such as the god of the wind). He left the earth, but left his technicians (High Priest) to operate the Ark so that He could keep track of the growth and development and food supply of this new species, but wars between developing tribes and groups resulted in the loss of the Ark. We truly lost touch with our creator. After hundreds, perhaps thousands of years with no communication from earth, a plan was hatched to reconnect with Earth when this planet reached its closest point to Earth. Given the war-like nature of the races that had developed on Earth, a stealth project was chosen; someone would live among this race of creatures to understand how they were developing. Yahweh decided that He, Himself, would take human form," he said.

"I don't understand where you are going with this, Dr. Goldberg," said Penny.

"Are you a Christian, Ms. Brooks?" he asked.

"Yes, although not a loyal churchgoer, I have believed the teachings of the Lutheran Church," she responded.

"But, you understand the Holy Trinity?" Goldberg asked.

"I cannot truly say that I understand it," she responded, "it is something that we take on faith."

"There was a big battle in the early Christian church, lead by Arius, who did not believe that Jesus was of the same 'substance' as Yahweh, His father. This battle was called 'Arianism' but should not be confused with Hitler's Aryanism. The movement proclaimed that a human being, as Jesus was, could not be of the same substance as Yahweh (a god); they were two separate and different beings. You see, by the time Jesus was born, Yahweh was no longer present and had become an omnipresent god, too large to be contained in a human-like body. He did walk the earth in Old Testament times, but He became the Holy Ghost - no longer incarnate, but was the father of Jesus. Yahweh did not mate with a woman to give birth to His child, but He mysteriously made an earth woman pregnant with His son. The early generations thought this was magic, or a miracle, later generations cannot believe it at all. It was really quite simple. It could not be described to people uneducated in the technology of a far more advanced civilization, so it wasn't, but anyone who had gained the knowledge of that technology would understand what really happened. For God (Yahweh) to take human form, he would have to clone himself (or use recombinant DNA technology) and plant that embryo in a woman host - Mary. There is no better description of *God, Made Man and a Virgin Birth*. Sex was not involved in the birth of Jesus. The 'angel' of the Lord impregnated (implanted the embryo) in Mary while she slept (probably induced or enhanced by the angel)," he said.

"That is a lot to accept, professor. I am sure that all Christians will have great difficulty accepting what you have just said," Penny responded.

"I have no doubt about that, Ms Brooks, but nothing that we have concluded attacks the BIBLE or what it says, it simply more clearly explains what the BIBLE is *really* saying. We cannot read the BIBLE with the eyes of a child; we are no longer children; we are an adult society that has discovered some of the tools in Yahweh's tool chest. We used to tell children that babies were delivered by a stork, but now, you can watch children on television kissing their mothers' bulging bellies and listening for sounds of the baby. Our society lacks the naivete for the stork to survive as the helpful creature it used to be. 'When I was a child I spake as a child, but it is time to put away childish things,' *Ja?* If this ancient biotechnology offends your sensibilities and seems preposterous, at first blush, go back to 'Genesis' and read about Melchizedek, the King of Salem. He is described as 'having never been born, and had no mother or father.' It sounds very much to me that Melchizedek sprang from Yahweh's test tube. Also, read the Book of Hebrews very carefully. The author is taking great pains to describe the difference between Melchizedek and Jesus as different life forms. Jesus is superior because he came from Yahweh's seed (Jesus His only 'begotten son'), while Melchizedek did not.

It has been a difficult journey for me, also, but I am more enthused about seeing my creator than I have ever been and I do not, necessarily, mean through death's door, but, perhaps the 'Second Coming.' I do hope to live until 2012 or 2013 A.D. to greet the race that created us," he said. Not so incidentally, I have even heard one of your great Christian ministers, a man called Billy Graham, quoted as saying that it would not surprise him to learn that the human race had been created by a far superior race from another planet in the universe. I hope that he will be able to shepherd a large flock through some of the difficulties that this material presents," Goldberg concluded.

"I presume," said Robert, "that you believe the resurrection was achieved through some technological marvel?"

"Yes, I do," responded Goldberg, "and that He then ascended to his father by means of some kind of teleportation device. It all sounds like something out of a modern science fiction book, doesn't it? But many scientific marvels of today were once science fiction; in the instance of the miracles described in the BIBLE, it could best be called 'science friction,' because science cannot accept that we have been visited in the ancient past. We feel that if we cannot find an ancient spaceship on earth, kick its tires, it could not have happened. I was once one of those scientists, but the BIBLE is the most magnificent footprint of ancient visitation....the very best evidence possible. It records the visit by these remarkable beings. It was written in such a way that it would have meaning to those of childlike faith, but contain technological truths that could be understood by a person of science or one familiar with scientific achievements. My God, we have been so blind! A virgin birth, a surrogate mother, reviving the dead are some of our own achievements of the past few decades! Perhaps on a smaller scale, but we are there - knocking on Yahweh's door!" he said with great fervor.

"There are many in the Christian world, Dr. Goldberg, who say that biotechnology and genetic engineering are the outright theft of

God's imprimatur. We have cloned animals and somewhere in the world someone is probably trying to clone a human. How would you respond to those with all that you have gleaned from your research into the Ark of the Covenant and its real purpose?" Penny asked.

"When people began to work together to build a tower, in ancient times, it troubled Yahweh so He had it destroyed. If He is able to monitor us and/or is truly omnipotent and did not want us to achieve our scientific breakthroughs, He would have blocked our progress. All governments of the world should put parameters on biotechnology, but it is a genie that will never be put back in the bottle. It offers too much hope for genetic therapies to cure the disorders and diseases that cause incalculable human suffering," he responded.

"What are your thoughts on human cloning, Dr. Goldberg?" asked Robert.

"You may not wish to publish what I am about to say. What I truly believe, based on the BIBLE and our research conclusions of sixty years ago, is that when we are able to record all of a human's memories - including those that constitute an individual's persona - we will have nearly completed the physics of immortality. Think about it. If I could clone my body, and upload (to use a computer term) those stored memories into the cloned body, I could be reborn - literally. I suggest that that has always been the real meaning of being *reborn* and *immortality.* The 'soul,' that not even the church can really define, is defined by science: it is the equivalent of a software program containing all memories that can be removed from one machine (body) and used in another. I believe the day is not too far distant when it will be as simple as that. Death will only come to those unworthy of being reborn: rapists, murderers and incorrigible thieves. Is that not the major article of the Christian belief?" he asked, rhetorically. "Have we not just glimpsed Yahweh's physics of immortality and how He and Jesus are One?"

"Wow! It certainly is a cogent and understandable path to immortality," said Robert, "and I can understand, now, why the Vatican government would go to extremes, to keep all of this under wraps, but they must know that the day of reckoning is coming. Why haven't they taken any steps to, what is the term I want, re-educate people to prepare them for the return of the planet (the 'Second Coming') of Yahweh and Jesus?" Robert asked.

"I cannot answer that. Perhaps they feel that ignorance is bliss or that the church would crumble, or more appropriately, crash if this information became public. The great charitable work done by the Vatican would suffer greatly. It would certainly be difficult to appeal for charitable contributions if the public knew that they had kept silent about the true nature of the Ark, when they have had that information

for over sixty years," Goldberg responded.

Robert said, "It would be a far worse scandal than sex abuse by the priests."

"Indeed, it would," replied the professor. Penny was pensive and Robert was concerned that the information had made her too uncomfortable. He was about to ask her if she was alright when Robert saw a red dot on the professor's chest. Robert knew, immediately, what he was seeing and he pulled the professor's chair away from the desk. "Get down!" he shouted, just as a bullet hit the bookshelf behind the professor's desk.

They were all prone, on the floor, as they waited for more bullets to fly above their heads, but nothing happened until they heard a door rattle somewhere towards the back of the house. The professor spoke, "Penny you get the phone; Robert, there is a gun in the center drawer of my desk. Hurry while he is still at the door! Penny handed the phone to Goldberg and Robert returned to the floor with the gun. Both were crawling on their hands and knees. Goldberg was talking excitedly to the police. He hung up the phone and said, "They will be here shortly. If we could crawl just around the door, there is a small laundry room that has no windows. We would be safe unless he breaks into the house. Then you will have to use the gun, Robert; I couldn't hit a thing unless it's right in front of my face." Robert took

the gun and all the legal ramifications of using it were rattling around in his head. It didn't matter, he was protecting life. He would do what he had to do. He was a decent shot although he hadn't been to the range in about a year. They heard the two-tone klaxon off in the distance as the shooter broke through the back door. They heard soft footsteps coming toward them. Robert could see the shooter, who was wearing a ski mask. He was tall and thin and dressed all in black. He spotted Robert and shot immediately, pushing Robert back into the laundry room. He was moving closer, and as he stood in the doorway, Robert took aim from behind the washing machine and fired. The man collapsed to the floor and they all stood and moved, almost in unison, toward the prone man. They heard the ear-splitting klaxon as the police pulled in front of the house.

The professor went to the front door and let the police into the foyer. He was explaining the circumstances as they were moving toward Goldberg's office. Penny was holding a towel she found in the laundry room over the wound in the shooter's shoulder. One of the policemen talked on a radiophone to call for an ambulance. The other one knelt down and pulled off the ski mask. Both Penny and Robert gasped; it was Timothy Witten. Robert could hardly contain his anger, "You son-of-a-bitch, I thought you were my friend! You were just hanging about to find out what Penny and I were up to. I should have put that bullet through your heart, you murderous swine! You would have killed us all, if you could have!"

Penny explained to the officers that she and Robert knew the shooter and what Robert had said. She turned to the professor and said, "I am so sorry, Professor. This is the grandson of Krueger. I thought that danger was past us, but I guess Karl Witten Jr. has inherited the manuscript from his father and the danger will not be over until we expose him and the manuscript," she said. "I will publish every word that you said, with your permission; this has to be over for all of us. It is the only way." The professor nodded his agreement. The ambulance arrived and one of the officers went with Witten to the *krankenhaus* (hospital), while Penny, Robert and the professor followed the other policeman, in the rented car, to the station to make their formal statements.

They were told that they could leave the country and the prosecutor for the city of Munich would contact the Manhattan prosecutor's office if they needed to make any further inquiries. Penny was concerned about Goldberg; would anyone else be sent to kill him? Was there any need since Witten would know that the meeting had taken place and his son was nearly killed for his failed effort? She thought he was probably safe, but that there might be a concerted effort to eliminate Robert and herself. They were really the only threat, now, to Witten's political campaign and election to the presidency. She would see him rot in hell before she would let *that* happen!

Robert had called the Manhattan prosecutor's office and made arrangements to be picked up by them as they disembarked from the plane. There would *not* be another shooting, another death, as they walked through JFK. They would be whisked away in an effort to spoil any planned attempt on their lives at the airport. They would be heavily guarded until Penny's book hit the bookstores. The district attorney had a safe house in Westchester County where he would house important witnesses until a trial date and decided, quickly, that both Robert and Penny would stay there until charges were formalized and Timothy Witten was extradited from Germany.

After Timothy Witten's trial Robert and Penny and Penny's grandparents returned to their interrupted lives. Senator Witten was given a strong warning by DA Mc Carthy that he would be watched, but all believed he would not dare take any action against the Penrose-Brooks family.

Chapter Fifteen

New York City
September 15, 2008

The book took much longer to write than Penny had hoped, but of course, a large church wedding and the birth of two children made a wonderful excuse. Their son, Anthony, was born on May 18, 2006, and their daughter, Angela was born on July 15, 2007.

When the book was published on October 15, 2008, it caused a tidal wave and forced Witten to throw his support to the conservative ticket. His resignation speech was masterful: 'sometimes the sins of the father must be atoned for by the son.' The blackmail of the Vatican was a terrible, terrible mistake. He apologized for a son who went too far in supporting his father's campaign for political office. He was young and foolish, but not a bad kid; he never intended to murder anyone, just frighten them. He and his family would retire from political life and spend their days in penitence and thankful for the opportunities that the American people had given them over the span of his political life.

Many of his campaign workers were crying; most felt he should have stayed in the campaign and let the voters decide, but Karl Witten Jr. would not run if he thought he could not win; his tremendous ego would not accept a defeat at the polls.

The Vatican had tried to remain silent on Penny's book, but the roar around the world would not permit such reticence. Finally, the pope issued a statement:

> "I do not know what my predecessor did with regard to the claim that the Vatican was blackmailed by Hitler and/or a Major Krueger. I have searched our records and there is no evidence that the Vatican ever paid any blackmail. With regards to the claim that Adolf Hitler found the Ark of the Covenant - we have no such knowledge and think that Ms. Brooks is given to hyperbole and flights of fantasy. We find the material in her book preposterous. How she got reputable scientists involved in such nonsense defeats even me."
>
> Signed,
>
> Pope Benedict XVI
> Citte del Vaticano

Those who truly wanted to believe the pope did so, but there were millions who could not so readily dismiss the gravitas of the scientists involved. Each one became an overnight superstar appearing on a variety of television shows with Penny. Even Artur Goldberg gave on-camera appearances from his home in Munich. He, singularly, changed millions of peoples' minds. He was a well-known physicist and told his personal story of how Hitler only kept him alive to work on this project. He had been taken from a prison camp to work on the analysis of the device known as the Ark of the Covenant and attested to the fact that Penny told his story with great integrity and there were no flights of fantasy in her book. Penny's book shot straight to the top of the New York Times bestseller list and stayed there for over a year.

She and Robert were extremely happy, but their lives had changed dramatically. They were bombarded with requests for personal appearances and decided they should hire a publicist and business manager. They had more money than they could spend in many lifetimes and were given good advice about establishing a foundation. There was another condo available in their building so they grabbed it up after assurances that there would be no difficulty using it for an office. Robert would head the foundation and decided to resign from the prosecutor's office, but would stay for a month and be available until all his cases were resolved.

Penny already had another book planned after she and Robert had many, many discussions with additional scientists. Penny was delighted that Robert remained an integral part of her professional life; his interest never seemed to wane. Their publicist and manager returned from a meeting with the exciting news that Neptune, a large movie production company, had offered an obscene amount of money for the movie rights to her book. Penny and Robert accepted the offer and were given the unusual right of script approval. Penny wanted to be sure that her grandparents and other people in the book were portrayed honestly.

Because their lives were so hectic, they had to hire a nanny, but Penny was determined that the nanny would not become a substitute mother. She and Robert took three breaks throughout the day to leave the office on the first floor to go to the penthouse to play and visit with the children.

The movie was a colossal success and faithful to the book. Penny never dreamed that she could ever achieve the professional success and the financial freedom the book and movie provided. She and her family could live a life of luxury for the rest of their days if she never did another thing, but that was not Penny. She had to work; it was as important to her as the food that nourished her body. She thought her work nourished her soul.

Robert went to a couple of meetings to see the people at the Simon Wiesenthal Center in California without Penny. She was putting the final touches on her second book. They both had discussed a sizable Foundation contribution to the center. Robert and Penny had several discussions about a large contribution to the Vatican. Penny respected the charitable works done by the church, but she was still steamed that they had told an outright lie to the world. Her personal embarrassment was long gone; Penny did not hold grudges, but she was terribly disappointed with the pope. She wasn't going to let him get away with it in her second book. She wondered if the contribution would be viewed as hypocritical. She wanted to help those causes the church supported; maybe they should just support the causes directly.

She had turned over the rough draft of her second book to the publisher so their legal department would have a head start on their work while she finished the final draft. Everything was going well until she returned to the penthouse one evening and found the nanny unconscious on the kitchen floor and no children to be found. Her heart was in her throat as she searched for the smelling salts to revive the nanny. It wasn't that simple. She called an ambulance and then got Robert on the intercom that they had installed between the penthouse and the office. He was there before the ambulance and called his former boss telling him their children had been kidnapped. Penny was near hysteria when the ambulance arrived. She and Robert followed the ambulance in their car and into the emergency room with the nanny. She had a fractured skull and wouldn't be telling them anything - she could be unconscious for days. The district attorney appeared, in person, and sent them back to their penthouse with two detectives who would be setting a trap on their phone to wait for a ransom demand. It was starting all over, again, but who? Witten wouldn't be involved unless it was just for revenge. It just did not seem likely. His son, Timothy, was spending 10 years in prison for attempted murder. Who else could it be? The Vatican? What could they hope to accomplish?

The call did not come until the following morning. Neither Penny nor Robert had slept a wink all night despite the tranquilizer a doctor had prescribed for Penny. Robert picked up the phone on the third ring, as directed. "Mr. West, we have both your children and they will die if you do not follow our instructions to the letter. We know there is a tap on your phone. If you want to see your children, again, leave your condo and go to a phone booth and call this number, 555-0123. It is a prepaid cell phone and no one will have time to triangulate the call. You have ten minutes from the time I hang up this phone to make that call. Don't be late; you will not like the consequences." The phone went dead. Robert looked at everyone and turned and ran to the elevator. There were phone booths in the lobby, but they were all engaged. Robert opened the door of one and grabbed the phone from an old lady. "I am sorry, Ma'am, this is a matter of life and death! I will not be long," he said.

Robert returned to the penthouse. "They want 20 million dollars and Penny has to make the drop. No husband. No cops. We have four hours to get the money, in one hundred dollar, unmarked bills, and make the drop at Grand Central Station. No gel paks. Penny is to leave the suitcases (they said there will be two required) next to the main ticket booth in the main lobby. She is to walk to the newspaper kiosk and is not to move until she sees the children walking toward her. That's it. I'll call the bank. If you guys (detectives) are going to be there you better get there as soon as possible. I suggest you change into casual clothes, I don't want them spotting you. Can you do this, Penny?" he asked.

"I will do whatever I have to do to get my children back," she said through her tears. She went to take a shower and to get dressed. In three hours the money was delivered to the penthouse by bonded courier. They signed and began packing the money into the two suitcases that Robert removed from the closet. They timed the drop-off so Penny would not have to wait more than ten minutes at the newspaper kiosk, after she placed the suitcases where instructed. Right on time she saw her two toddlers heading in her direction. She was about to run to meet them when she was grabbed from behind.

One of the detectives retrieved the children while the other tried to follow where the kidnappers had taken Penny. He lost the trail in the lobby of the Grand Hyatt. They could have gotten her onto a train, hidden her in one of the hotel rooms or grabbed a car or cab in front of the hotel entrance. She was gone! They should have had more people, but they were afraid of being spotted! What was this? Did they plan to kidnap Penny all along and the children were taken just to make the switch? Who was behind this? Why did they need her once they had the ransom money? Would they receive a call for more money?

Chapter Sixteen

Penny didn't have any idea where she was. Even though she had been drugged, she had been semi-conscious enough to know that she was on a plane; she could feel the vibration. Who had her? The Vatican? Someone connected with Witten? What could he hope to accomplish, now, except to kill her out of revenge? They could have killed her at any time, they did not need to fly her to some other part of the country. It was hard to hold a thought in her head for very long; the drug was too powerful.

She felt water splashed on her face and she awoke to a group of young men who appeared Semitic. She was pulled to her feet and led, with one man holding each arm, to exit the aircraft. It was a Lear jet. She felt a wave of heat as she was led down the steps of the airplane and sensed she was somewhere in the Middle East. Palestinians or Israelis? Why, for heaven's sake? There was a black limousine waiting and she and her two guards were whisked away.

"Where am I and why have you kidnapped me? I gave you the money, what more do you want?" she asked in anger. There was no response, not even a reaction on the faces of the men. She knew she wasn't going to get any information from them. It seemed forever, but the ride only lasted about thirty minutes as they pulled in front of a large, resplendent house somewhere in the desert. Despite the dry heat, there was luscious green plant life and climbing clematis on one side of the house. It looked like an oasis in the desert. She was led to the front door where a maid took her to an inner part of the house; the guards had left her. She was told to make herself comfortable on one of the large sofas (there were three arranged around a large coffee table) and was served a large glass of iced tea. She was glad for the ice and had drunk half of the glass when she heard footsteps approaching. She was absolutely startled to see the man who entered the living room; it was the prime minister of Israel.

"Ms. Brooks," he said in heavily accented English, "I am sorry that you have not been told what has happened in the last twelve hours, but we followed what we believed to be the best course of action based on the information that we had, at the time." He paused to get her response.

"I do not understand, Mr. Eckstein, other than being kidnapped from my family and my country, what has transpired in the past twelve

hours and what right do you think you have to do such a thing? My husband must be frantic!"

"As soon as we finish our conversation, you may call your husband, but first let me explain the reason why I authorized this action. Your children were kidnapped by an extreme faction within the terrorist organization known as Hezbollah. We intercepted communications and learned of this plot only 24 hours ago. It was the reason *why* this kidnapping was to take place that prevented me from trying to work through official channels to prevent the planned action. Instead, I authorized a group of Israel's finest covert operators to locate this group to spoil their plans. They arrived too late to prevent the kidnapping of your children, but they were able to locate the group in New York City and were instructed to foil the second part of their plan and to bring you safely to me," he said. "We knew the second part of their plan was to take place at your Grand Central Station in New York City."

"Do you mean to say that they always intended to kidnap me?" asked Penny.

"Yes, your children would not have been kidnapped if they had found you at your home, but it was always their fall-back position, if they could locate the children. It was always you that they wanted."

"I don't understand why they would want me? I thought it was

the money that they wanted," she remarked.

"Oh, the money was only a fringe benefit. They want you to tell them where the Ark of the Covenant is located. They believe you have been withholding that information to keep your readers interested in your next book," he said.

"But I don't know where it is located. I said that in my first book!" exclaimed Penny.

"They don't believe you. They think that if they can get their hands on the Ark that they will be able to make the world to, what is it you say - sit up and take notice? They believe that they would then have the power that Hitler had - to blackmail the world," he said; "if they could get their hands on it, they could be right. For the security of my country, I had to learn if you do know more than you have said. Do you understand what I am saying, Ms. Brooks?" he asked.

"Yes, I understand, Mr. Prime Minister, but you did not have to kidnap me to ask that question," she said.

"Please understand that we foiled your kidnapping by Hezbollah. You would have been tortured mercilessly until they learned that you do not have that information. You would not have survived their methods, Ms. Brooks. We only brought you here to satisfy ourselves that you do not have that information and to devise a plan to prevent further attempts to kidnap you. We even recovered the money that you were required to pay as ransom. The two suitcases are in my gardening shed at the back of the house. They were flown here with you. We have no interest in your money," he said.

"I am sorry, Mr. Prime Minister, if I do not sound grateful. The last twenty-four hours have been horrendous for my family. I would give my life to save my children, but I do not wish to contemplate what would have happened to me in the hands of Hezbollah. Thank you for the resources you must have used to save my life. I will gladly reimburse your government for any expense you incurred," she said.

"That is not necessary, Ms Brooks; as I said it is a matter of state security. Is there anything more that you can tell me about the Ark? Do you still believe that it is in the hands of the people who were working with Ante Pavelic during the war? Do you think that it is probably lost, again?" he asked.

"No, Mr. Prime Minister, I do not think that it is lost. I believe that it is the hands of a Franciscan Order that worked hand-in-hand with Pavelic and the Croatian government. It was even said that this order was in charge of one of the prison camps in *Croatia* - the Jasenovac Camp. Can you imagine such a thing? Pavelic's small regime was one of the most brutal in human history; even the Germans showed more mercy, if you can believe that! I do have my doubts that the Vatican government knows anything about its location. This is a flank of a Franciscan Order that, I believe, operates independently of the Vatican. They are an autonomous order - true renegades," she finished.

"Do you understand that the Ark of the Covenant belongs to the Jewish people? It was left on earth with the ancient Jewish priesthood," he said.

"I understand its historical connection to the Jewish people, but I think it belongs to the world, don't you, Sir?" she asked. "Do you believe that only the Jewish people were created by the ancient god, Yahweh?" she asked.

"No, of course not!" he bridled.

"It is my interpretation that the Jewish people were chosen to operate the Ark, perhaps because you most closely followed the dictates or commandments regarding its operation, but, I must be honest - I think your ancient priesthood did a great disservice to the human race by not disclosing its true purpose; even after it was lost. The ancient priesthood appears to be very much like computer operators of a few decades ago who tried to talk in a private language that others could not understand. They were possessive of a knowledge that they tried to keep among themselves. It worked until the invention of the personal computer that everyone learned to operate. They lost some of their power and glory. The ancient priesthood kept secret a lot of information that has been nearly lost and recorded only in ancient texts that have been inaccessible to the masses. I find that irresponsible," she said.

"I must agree, Ms. Brooks. I cannot argue with anything that you have said, and not so incidentally, I think you have done a great service to mankind recovering this lost knowledge. We Jews did not accept Jesus as the Son of God, but I understand, now, why we did not and how we were wrong. You do agree that, even now, many will have difficulty with the concept, even with the clarity that you have brought to the concept of the Holy Trinity. To bear hatred for the Jewish people, today, for something done by our forefathers is also wrong. Just as modern Americans are not responsible for bringing Negroes from Africa for slave labor; it was done by their forefathers who did not recognize the full humanity of this race. For heaven's sake, Jesus *was* a Jew, he was not a Roman, Frenchman or an Englishman! He did not come to start the Christian church; that was created long after his death. Please explain to the Christians the history of their Christian church; they won't learn the history for themselves - maybe you can teach them through your work!" he was vehement.

"Do you have anymore questions for me, Mr. Prime Minister? I would like to call my husband," she said.

"Just one more question, Ms Brooks; do you think that the Ark is operational? That its holders are able to communicate with this distant planet?" he asked.

"I seriously doubt that Hitler would have returned the device in working order; it would take away some of the power that he sought to have for himself. I think that if it is ever recovered, you will find some piece missing that is necessary for it to function properly. A working model of this device *was* created by Hitler's scientists, but I suspect that it was destroyed during the war or some of Hitler's devotees would be using it to seek political favor somewhere in the world. The only thing that remains is to build a new device from the reverse-engineering documents provided by Dr. Goldberg. That is the project that my husband and I are working on with several scientists in my country. But, I would like to return, under more pleasant circumstances, to discuss this and some of the Jewish legends that may add more information as to when this device has the best chance of communicating with a distant planet. I believe that information is there, in your legends and, perhaps, holidays. Perhaps you could even suggest the best Jewish scholars that would be amenable to working on this project?" she asked.

"I will give that some thought, Ms. Brooks. Go, call your husband and then you will be flown back to your home. Please contact me when you wish to go further with your project - I will have names for you. My government would be very interested in being involved in this project - if you need additional funding, please let me know. I would appreciate an occasional up-date, if you are willing to share information?" he finished with a question mark.

"I would be happy to keep you updated. But, how are we going to keep Hezbollah away from my family? You alluded to some plan?"

"Would you be willing to let me tell the world, that Israel is in possession of the Ark? It would close the door on Hezbollah and any other terrorist's plan and give you time to work on your project. I think it might give us all a little peace of mind," he said.

"I have no difficulty with your idea, but won't your people demand to see it?" she asked.

"We can always say that it is being studied by our scientists, etc. It might also help to flush out those who were affiliated with Pavelic during the war and think *they* are its rightful owner. What do you think?" he asked.

"As long as you are willing to take any associated risks, I have no objection," Penny said.

"Good. We will make an announcement in the next few days. In the meantime, arrange for security guards at your home and office. Again, I apologize for my tactics in bringing you here, but it was necessary," he finished.

"I understand and accept your apology," she responded. He led her to the telephone and waited for her to finish. One hour later she was back on the plane, with two suitcases worth twenty million dollars and eating the first meal she had had in over 36 hours. She was famished and feasted on lamb chops. If she was tipsy this time, it would be due to the excellent wine that accompanied the meal. The arrival was uneventful and Robert was waiting with a limousine and three security guards. The district attorney had arranged for a customs officer to inspect her luggage on the plane - he was fully informed of the nature of her luggage and arrival from Israel.

Penny learned on the drive from the airport to her condo on Fifth Avenue that Nina, their nanny, was conscious and doing well. Robert had a temp taking care of the children, who were also under heavy guard. She had explained all about the circumstances of her trip to Israel and all that was said. Robert thought the announcement that the prime minister was willing to make with regard to the Ark of the Covenant was a great idea. It would take the pressure off while they finished their research and development project. Maybe they could get back to a normal life. He had been unable to touch food since Penny went missing. They would stay in the condo and eat and sleep until Israel made its announcement.

The children squealed, at the top of their little voices, when

Penny walked through the door. Robert did not dare tell them that he was picking up their mother at the airport, in case something went wrong. They all hugged in a circle as Penny cried. For a while, she thought she would never see them again; would not live to see them grow up.

It was two days later when Robert got the paper from outside the front door that he spotted the article on the lower section of the front page of the newspaper:

> Tel Aviv, AP
>
> The Israeli government announced, yesterday, that it has recovered a device that is believed to be the Ark of the Covenant that was lost during the second destruction of the Temple of Solomon. This device has received some notoriety in the past two years through the highly successful book, THE GENESIS COVERUP, by Penelope Brooks. The device was found in what is now *Croatia*, in roughly the location alluded to in Ms Brooks' book. The government has stated that it will take some time for it's scientists to study the device, but sources close to the prime minister have said that he is very excited by this find and hopes that modern technology will aid in determining its true purpose.

Robert rushed to the bedroom to wake Penny to read the article. When she finished, she said, "That's a relief. Maybe we will be able to work with him, after all. I have never really trusted politicians, but he kept his word and even gave me credit in the article. There can be no doubt that he has his motive, which is pretty clear; if we get this thing built and working, he wants his government to be the recipient of the technology. What do you think about that, Bobby?" (She was the only one who could call him that!)

"As long as he doesn't expect an exclusive right to the technology, I don't see a problem. That may be why he offered help with the financing; maybe he does want exclusive rights," he said as he turned toward Penny.

"Well, that's not going to happen, but we don't have to worry about that problem for awhile. We'll wait until we have a proto-type to cross that bridge," she replied.

"Did you hear anything from my publisher while I was gone?" she asked.

"Oh, I forgot with all that was happening. He said to tell you he loved the rough draft and the legal team gave a thumbs-up. Full speed ahead. He wants to know if you can have the final draft in three months," Robert replied.

"Geez! Give me a break!" she replied.

Chapter Seventeen

June 26, 2009
Lake George, New York

Penny's grandmother died of a stroke and her grandfather died of a heart attack within three months of her death. In truth, Penny knew that her grandfather died of a broken heart. He and Giselle had never spent more than a day apart since they were reunited after the war; he simply could not wait to rejoin her wherever she was. Penny doubted that there were many couples who enjoyed the same depth of love as her grandparents. Even in his eighties, her grandfather's eyes would light-up when Giselle entered the room and Giselle always reached for Laurence's arm or hand when walking together. Penny prayed that she and Robert would share that same depth of love. Typically, Laurence had already made the funeral arrangements with burial in a small cemetery in Lake George. After weeks of mourning, Penny had to redouble her efforts to get her second book completed by the promised date. She decided to do the final draft of her second book at Lake George. It would be the first time that she spent any amount of time there since her grandparents died. Her heart ached for them; they had been the center of her being for so many years. She was so happy that they had lived long enough to see her married and to know their great-grandchildren. It was probably comforting for them to know that Penny, now, had Robert and the children.

The children were only two and three, but they were old enough to love the oldest part of The Great Escape; when Penny was growing up and spending her summers at Lake George, its predecessor was known as Storytown, USA with all the cartoon characters that became so much a part of a child's life.

The chalet had been refurbished and Robert had attended to the refurnishing while she wrapped-up some business in the city; she would be joining him next week. She wanted to take the children to the theme park before the summer crowd overran the park and the lake. She was really looking forward to the slower pace of the Adirondacks to finish the book.

Penny arrived the last week of June and was astounded at the renovation work Robert had supervised and was delighted with the way he had furnished the place. Despite the changes and some of the newness, she still felt her grandparents' presence. It was not a sad feeling, but comforting in a way.

She thought back to four years ago when this incredible journey began with the attacks on her grandparents; it changed her on so many levels. She would never have met Robert without the events they had all experienced and doubted that she would have been able to face them all alone, especially the loss of her grandparents.

Robert had another big surprise for her. They walked down to the lakefront and she spotted it immediately - a large houseboat named "The Covenant" which she thought was appropriate on so many different levels: the keeping of the covenant with her grandparents by bringing her grandmother's tormentor to justice (his suicide was still a fitting end), the covenant between she and Robert and the covenant that she had made with her readers - to explain the truths behind the Ark of the Covenant as best she could understand them and even, perhaps, the covenant with those who would come someday to explain it better than she could.

They were walking back to the chalet when she spotted someone she thought she would never see, again; someone she hoped she would never see, again. Karl Witten Jr. was walking to his car. What was he doing in Lake George? Would the world never be rid of the Krueger/Wittens? Maybe he was just a tourist like many of the other people who had already invaded the small resort village.

"Bobby, I want to follow Witten, I think we should see where he goes. Do you think he is just visiting the lake, or, God forbid, did he retire here? Hurry up, he's moving away!" she urged. They followed

Witten's Chrysler from Bolton Landing to a motel right in the village. If he was staying at a motel maybe he *was* just visiting, but Penny was determined to keep track of his movements. She could not be comfortable knowing this son of a monster was in her backyard. Robert agreed that they should take turns watching his movements. Penny could sit in a car with her laptop computer and work on the book and monitor the motel. Nina, the nanny would watch the children while she slept and Robert took his shift during the nighttime hours. It was the third day before Witten's routine changed; it looked as if he was checking-out of the motel. He was packing the trunk of the car. Penny followed his car to the Northway entrance. She drove back to the motel and went to the office to dig for a little information.

"Excuse me, Miss, was that Senator Witten that I just saw leaving?" she asked.

"Why, yes, it was," she replied, "he is a partner in the business and the nephew of the co-owner; he comes back every year for a week or so."

"Thank you! Have a nice day," replied Penny as she turned quickly and bumped into someone waiting to register. She left and headed home anxious to tell Robert the news that Witten was gone, but also, that he had family running a business at the lake that he also co-owned.

Penny was sure that Witten inherited the manuscript from his father and wondered if he was putting some plan together to make use of this legacy. Could he make another bid for the White House after the public's shock of his father's background faded from public memory? It never seemed to take long for the public to forgive and/or forget the high crimes and misdemeanors of their public officials (even though Witten Jr.'s actual crime was still in the making). Would he try to get back into the senate? He had a lot of supporters and he had inherited a tremendous (ill-gotten) fortune from his father.

Penny gave the final draft of her second book her full attention and by the end of the summer the family headed back to New York City with her work completed. Her publisher was happy, so she was happy. The book was scheduled for release in the fall.

Robert came home one night in November and told Penny that the proto-type of the Ark was finished and a test was scheduled for the following week. She had kept her promise and kept the prime minister of Israel informed of their progress, so she called and asked if he wanted to be present at the test. He said that he would fly in the day before the test and would let her know when he arrived. They had also informed the government of the test and the director of NASA would represent the government and was instrumental in selecting the test site and projected path of the laser beam so as not to interfere with satellites and other NASA space projects. It was going to be an exciting moment. Dr. David MacIntyre had been invaluable in putting together a top-notch team of scientists to build this prototype and they were as excited as Penny and Robert to determine if this duplicate of the Ark (the same duplicate that Hitler had built based on Goldberg's work) would work. Several in-house tests confirmed that the external plates, those believed to duplicate those housed with the laser, were indeed capable of electrophoresis (the separation of blood into its component parts) and also an electron microscope capable of telecommunicating its images.

Penny found it ironic that here they were, two days after Thanksgiving, November 28, 2009, exactly the same day that Hitler had tested his reverse-engineered Ark fifty-seven years ago. It wasn't planned that way; could there be an unseen guiding hand? She couldn't help but wonder. So much of her long-held skepticism about visitors from unknown planets had slipped away over the past few years. If the renowned Artur Goldberg, physicist extraordinaire, had lost his doubts, how could *she* still question? Would this test bring new probes to earth? Would they be as passive as those "foo fighters" during World War II?

The test would take place, at midnight, on Hunter Mountain in the Helderbergs in Greene County, New York State, away from the light pollution of all cities. It would give a clearer view of the power of the laser beam. Penny and Robert donned thermal underwear beneath their jeans and parkas; the weather had already turned cold with a dusting of snow on the ground. It was a crystal clear night, just perfect for their purpose. Penny and Robert rode to the site in a limousine also carrying the prime minister of Israel and the director of NASA. There were three SUVs carrying the Ark and the scientists, headed by Dave Mac Intyre, who would be conducting the test. All were happy with the six large thermoses of coffee that Penny passed around with a stack of styrofoam cups. At exactly midnight, the Ark was activated and the beam was one of the most incredible sights Penny had ever seen. It seemed to go up into space forever and had a much wider beam than Penny expected. The sober and staid scientists were jumping up and down and slapping each other on the back like a high school football team that had just won the biggest playoff of their lives. Their joy was infectious. The laser beam was left on for thirty minutes and, just before the scheduled completion of the experiment, a large orange ball of fire appeared adjacent to the bluish-white light of the beam. It just stayed there. Penny heard several "Holy s--ts!" All agreed to keep the laser on for another fifteen minutes and just before the planned shut-down the orange light disappeared as if it knew the jig was up. Everyone was astounded. "Someone" or "something" was definitely "out there."

Neither the director of NASA nor the prime minister had much to say on the drive back to the city. Everyone seemed lost in his own thoughts. Even with the car heater at full blast, everyone was still cold, probably intensified by the shock of what they had just seen; it was also very late. They all agreed to meet for lunch at the Foundation's office at 12 o'clock later that day; it was already 2:30 in the morning. Penny left a note for Nina to call the caterer they frequently used, to arrange for lunch for twelve and delivery by 12 noon at the Foundation's office on the first floor of their building.

Dave MacIntyre and his seven cohorts arrived at 11:45AM, and the prime minister arrived shortly thereafter, but there was no sign of the director of NASA. They were about to sit down to lunch when the office phone rang and it was the director apologizing; he would be unable to attend, but would appreciate hearing what the scientists thought they had seen during the experiment. The meeting went on for most of the afternoon as the scientists kicked around thoughts about the large orange object. It was concluded that it was between 200-300 feet in diameter and conformed to some of the descriptions some had pulled-off the internet of modern UFO sightings. One of the scientists was assigned the task of researching the descriptions of the "foo fighters" during World War II and had his laptop computer open at two websites. He discovered a sighting over Turin, Italy in 1942 and another over Essen, Germany in 1943 during a bombing raid on the Krupps Armament Works that conformed to what they had all seen in the wee hours of the morning. The object had oscillated between a cigar, metallic looking object to a large orange ball of fire that positioned itself at a 45° angle. Many of the scientists were being exposed to the UFO phenomenon for the first time and appeared truly shaken. None had ever believed any of the numerous reports of UFO flaps that occasionally crop-up in the news. The comfortable conclusion that it was the misinterpretation of natural phenomena did not fit anymore; they had seen this 'thing' with their own eyes! The experiment they were conducting from the device *they* had engineered caused it to appear! They began to sympathize with those individuals who had the courage to report these sightings, but were met with stony silence or, worst - humiliation by agencies of the federal government. Based on what they knew, now, the very first sighting of these unknown objects first appeared, in the modern era, in the fall of 1942, but one of the group believed there was descriptive evidence of similar phenomena in the BIBLE. Whether it was Hitler's experiment with the device (that they all now knew, for certain, *was* the Ark of the Covenant), or merely the war, itself, that attracted 'someone's' attention, they could not be sure.

The meeting broke-up at four o'clock, although it could have gone on for many more hours. Dave MacIntyre had to get back to his office at Columbia University for meetings he had scheduled with several students. The Ark (the modern version) was locked in a large walk-in vault at the university that had been especially built for the device and paid for by the Penrose-Brooks Foundation. It was seven feet tall, seven feet wide and seven feet deep and weighed nearly seven tons. It was waterproof, and could withstand anything except perhaps a direct hit by a nuclear bomb. It is important to understand the precautions taken to protect the Ark because when Dave MacIntyre got back to his office, it was a wreck! He immediately took the elevator to the sub-basement where the Ark was housed, but it was undisturbed. Dave immediately called Penny and then called the security office at the university to report the incident and arrange for further security measures. If there were any further incidents, Penny would arrange for a private security force, but she was nonplussed. Was Dave's office ransacked by a student looking for answers to an up-coming test? No one, except the people who were part of the experiment, knew about Dave's participation. That wasn't exactly true - both the director of NASA and the prime minister of Israel could have reported that Dave was the project manager to other individuals in their respective governments. Witten had no way of knowing, did he? Could one of his friends in the government have notified him about the experiment and Dave's participation?

The next two weeks passed with no further incidents and another test was scheduled for the following week. There were now several inches of snow on the ground from a recent storm, but the roads were well maintained and the climb up Hunter Mountain was uneventful. The same people were in attendance with the exception of the prime minister, who had to cancel due to an upswing in terrorist activity in his homeland. He seemed truly disappointed that he could not attend, but Penny promised a full report. As the laser was activated, those present were treated to a spectacular light show. The large orange object broke into six smaller objects and their colors oscillated between all the colors of the spectrum. It was awesome - and absolutely inexplicable. Penny studied the faces of the scientists and saw awe and fear in equal measure. The six objects zoomed across the sky at incomprehensible speeds, dipped close to the earth and flew to heights that took them beyond human vision. It was impossible to follow them with a telescope; it took longer to reposition the telescope than it took an object to return to its original position or disappear from view. They were about to shut the laser down when they were given another surprise; one of the smaller objects flew to within five-hundred feet and stayed. Many were busy with their digital cameras. It seemed to know that the scientists needed to see it close enough for more careful study. After a couple of minutes, the recombined other objects flew to within the five-hundred feet and picked-up the straggler, like a mother duck retrieving a wayward duckling and it flew beyond their vision in what seemed to Penny to be nano seconds. How was this possible? It seemed to Penny that the incredible speed would kill any human-like being aboard. Was this an unmanned probe of some kind?

Penny could hardly wait for the follow-up meeting later that day. She had slept very little with the dozens of questions buzzing around inside her head. Would the photographs taken be able to answer some of these questions? Dave turned on his laptop and connected the cable to a large screen in the Foundation's boardroom that would allow them all to see the dozens of pictures taken. There were seventy-two pictures that he went through rather quickly to give many their first view then returned to the beginning to go through them one at a time to squeeze-out every bit of information through discussion with the whole group.

"Dave," spoke Marshall Montgomery, the aero-engineer of the group, "there is definitely a disc in the center of each ball of light. My guess is that each individual ball contains a hard disc with a diameter of around fifty feet. That disc conforms to many UFO historical sighting reports I have read in the past few days. What I find most interesting is when they recombine to form a cigar shape. I am truly at a loss trying to comprehend this shape changing," he finished.

"Marshall," spoke Penny, "what do you think about the idea that these small objects are like individual cars in a train that can operate individually, under certain circumstances, but have to reconnect to the equivalent of the train's locomotive for perhaps longer distance traveling. We are talking about some kind of spaceship, aren't we?"

"I believe we are Ms. Brooks, and I think that is a wonderful interpretation of what we witnessed; a futuristic space train - I love it! One view is of the individual cars and the other looks like a cigar; perhaps a better description would be like a 'bullet' train. It's perfect! I think we are lucky to have your analytical skills on the team, Ms. Brooks; we have just taken a giant step toward understanding this part of the phenomenon," he said.

"What about these incredible speeds, Mark? Any idea what is propelling these things?" asked Robert.

"I have no idea what kind of distance these things have traveled to get here, but I can't help but wonder if our laser is somehow opening some kind of door for them. They just appear out of nowhere, right next to the beam. Do you understand what I am saying, Dave?"

"I do, but cannot imagine the technology involved. Are you suggesting some kind of resonance, for the lack of a better word, with the light amplification of the laser, or that the laser is opening a hole in space for them to enter?" asked Dave.

"I could not have articulated it any better; yes, I guess that is what I am saying," responded Mark.

"Back to the speed," said Robert, "how can any kind of spaceship, traveling at those tremendous speeds stop on a dime like those we witnessed? The G-force would kill any human being or similar creature wouldn't it?

"Yes, it would," responded Mark. "The only thing that makes any kind of sense, within the known laws of physics, is that each ship has its own atmosphere, probably continually creates it through some kind of chamber that mixes the gases required and propels it outside and around the whole ship; I am not sure what binds the atmosphere to the ship, but I can begin to see how that might be possible, but the technology is way, way beyond us. It's a truly remarkable achievement. Whoever has created this technology is years and years ahead of any futuristic vision that I have ever heard about on our planet and I watch developments around the world. This is not an earthly creation; we are watching the technological achievements of a superior civilization."

"I have been researching the reports about this phenomena and descriptions of these little gray beings," said Robert. "Have any of you read about them and reached any conclusions?"

Dan Holloway had studied under astronomer and exo-biologist, Carl Sagan, and spoke up: "Yes, lay people think they are an extraterrestrial race, but it is my opinion that these are genetically engineered creatures that are actually an integral part of the structure of the ship, itself. We (earthlings) used to send animals in space in the early days of space programs; whoever is behind these creatures have, I believe, genetically designed their 'animals,' programmed them as pilots and, I guess, genetic researchers, if even one of these abduction reports is true," finished Dan.

Again, the meeting went on all afternoon and some ideas were beginning to harden in the minds of those involved. Another test would take place in a month, giving those involved a needed break to concentrate on their normal full-time duties. Penny spent most of that evening putting the day's discussion into some semblance of a report. After the attempted robbery, or whatever it was, at Dave's university office, Penny and Robert tightened their own security measures and kept all of the Ark research material in a large safe in the Foundation's office and had a laser security system installed. No matter the hour, Penny would take whatever documents or notes she was working on and return the material to the safe three floors below.

At four o'clock the following morning the telephone rang. It was the security guard calling from the ground floor informing her that someone had attempted to break-in to the Foundation office. She and Robert grabbed their clothes and took the elevator to the ground floor where the security guard was waiting. The glass door to the Foundation's office had been shattered, but the burglar had been scared away. The security guard was just returning from his rounds of the building when he heard the glass break and saw the burglar take flight when the alarm sounded; the burglar had never entered. Now, what, thought Penny!

They were on their way back to their condo when Robert finally spoke and said to Penny, "I think someone in the government is behind this break-in and the break-in at Dave's office."

"*Our* government! Why do you think that?" was her immediate inquiry. We have included NASA in this project. Why would they need to steal our reports?" she asked.

"I think NASA has told someone else in the government about the Ark and our project; someone who wants to know more about our experiments," responded Robert.

"Who do you think? Isn't the CIA the usual culprit? I thought they had cleaned-up their act and didn't do these kind of 'black bag' type jobs anymore," Penny responded.

I think you mean 'black op' kind of jobs, Dear; I am not sure 'why,' except to say that the ability to 'call' these 'visitors,' has had to have made anyone who knows about this phenomenon and has been able to successfully deny it pretty concerned. Just stop and think about the thousands, if not millions of people who have reported this phenomenon for decades and have been humiliated by governmental agencies labeling them 'crackpots,' because they could not admit that they had no power to stop what was happening and could not even begin to explain it. They cannot let non-governmental people explain it and control any communication that we might eventually have through our experiments; we might be the ones to make the real first contact with another intelligent species - maybe even our creator(s). This may be where our experiments will lead. We may be awakening a sleeping, dangerous giant; and I don't mean whatever is out there, I mean in our very own government. We may be bumping up against the equivalent of the ancient, conservative Jewish priesthood who refused to accept Jesus' divinity and the nature of his birth because to do so would expose their crime - 'the Genesis Cover-up' - the withholding of the true nature of our origin from the masses. . . the biotechnology that created us and created Jesus. Information that should have been preserved for all humanity; but, when the Ark was lost this ancient priesthood thought of their own power first. The sacrifice that was supposed to be pleasing to God, was now pleasing to the priesthood. That is why Jesus turned over the moneychangers tables in the temple.

This money bought animals for sacrifice - a sacrifice that had lost its purpose with the loss of the Ark. No wonder Jesus was livid at this practice!

We are a threat to many different groups. We have to analyze, in detail, who to approach in the government, probably at a higher level than the director of NASA while protecting ourselves from other self-interest groups, especially religious groups who feel threatened by this discovery," he concluded.

"Wow, Bobby! That's a mouthful and you are absolutely right. Let's get showered and I'll make a big pot of coffee; by the end of the day, we will know what we have to do," she said.

The salient points were pretty easy to summarize; from the Old Testament to the New Testament, the temple and churches were promulgating a misinterpreted version of events in biblical history. We, now, had the framework to understand this ancient (and present) phenomenon. As the BIBLE says, 'when I was a child, I spake as a child, but the time has come to put away childish things.' What has been viewed as supernatural phenomena can, now, be understood within the laws of physics (or, at least, some of the phenomena):

1) The ancient Jewish priesthood (the first governing body on earth) withheld the knowledge that the Ark of the Covenant was our telecommunication link to a superior race of *immortals* that created us

and continued to monitor our growth and development. The early priesthood was the protector and operator of a device (the Ark) and its function. When the Ark was lost, in war, this fact was never explained to the trusting masses that continued to bring their animals to the 'temple' (for sacrifice) to be tested. As the *immortals'* planet moved out of the solar system to the far reaches of the Oort Cloud, communication was lost and nothing could be done from the *immortals'* end to re-establish contact for a very long time. Although small bits of information could be found in ancient legend to suggest that today's religious interpretation of the Ark is erroneous, only the recreation or reverse-engineering of the object proved the horrendous enormity of this *cover-up.* Someone, schooled in the deep mysteries of the Jewish religion, was needed to serve as a counselor and interpreter with the research group. The prime minister of Israel should be consulted for his opinion on who should be chosen to join the research group.

2) The birth of Jesus, introduced by the *Star of Bethlehem*, and the story of a virgin birth and the eventual death and *resurrection* of *God Incarnate* (god, made man) was an attempt by our *creator(s)* to reconnect with earth and explain the *technology* that would make each and everyone (who was law abiding) an *immortal.* Jesus' death was *essential* to *prove* this technology worked, but when few in leadership roles accepted what Yahweh/Jesus tried to offer all humanity - the plan

was abandoned - earth was left in darkness once again, but Jesus left with the promise to return (when the planet of His Father returned to the solar system) to see if we would be ready to accept the technology of this superior race. Someone, schooled in the deep mysteries of the Christian religion, was needed to serve as a counselor with the research group. It was probably pointless to contact the Vatican See after the pope's ridicule of Penny's book, but perhaps someone with a good relationship with the Catholic church could make contact through a cardinal or bishop in New York City. An approach should be made with the evangelist, Billy Graham, or his son, given the failing health of his father, to see if either would be amenable to serving as a consultant with the research group.

3) The federal government has, for at least 60 years, been denying the existence of the UFO phenomenon. Even scientists serving on the early Project Blue Book investigating this phenomenon had no 'framework' with which to understand what they or private individuals were seeing or from where these 'vehicles' may be coming. The research group could help to provide this framework if an open-minded government official would be willing to work with the research group. Penny remembered reading where a former CIA director had made some intelligent remarks about the phenomenon and wondered if they should try to approach him.

No matter what cooperation they got from the religious groups mentioned or the government, Penny would continue to inform her readers about the continuing revelations from operation of the reverse-engineered Ark.

Chapter Eighteen

Rabbi Minkowski was a Polish Jew who had survived the holocaust and despite his advanced years (as old as Penny's grandfather), he had a young spirit and an open, inquiring mind. We agreed to meet with him in Israel so that he could determine whether he wanted to make the trip to the United States to work with the Penrose-Brooks Foundation. He was highly recommended by the prime minister of Israel for his knowledge of Jewish legend and seventy-five years of scholarship with regard to the Jewish Torah. He was a retired professor of comparative religions from the Hebrew University of Jerusalem. His wife was deceased and his children lived in the United States which was a big plus in his accepting a consulting position that would bring him closer to his children, grandchildren and great-grandchildren who he only saw once a year, if that often. There were years when terrorist activity kept them all away from Israel.

As agreed, Penny would conduct most of the interview, but

Robert would help out if needed, "Rabbi, have you been told about the project that Hitler instituted during World War II? The project to recreate the Ark of the Covenant by reverse-engineering a device that was actually found in Croatia?"

"Oh, better than that, Ms. Brooks, I have read your book, THE GENESIS COVERUP! I am not a stuffy, old professor. I know Artur Goldberg, too. He was a visiting professor at the university when he was still able to travel. We got together and discussed some of our shared experiences during the war and we still communicate. I do not doubt what he has told you about this project. He is a man of great integrity, so I have to take what you have written most seriously. The concept that a superior race of beings came from another planet to our planet and created homo sapiens does not, in any way, conflict with the teachings of the Torah or the Christian BIBLE, for that matter. Just because you may have a good idea where that planet is and have determined that the Ark of the Covenant was the way to communicate with this race of beings changes nothing. It merely explains, in better detail, what most of us have accepted on faith. I have always thought that the day would come when faith would be rewarded - that we would be able to comprehend with our god-given intelligence what we have had to accept with our hearts," he seemed to wind down.

"Rabbi Minkowski, do you think that the modern UFO

phenomenon could be ushering in the 'Second Coming?' asked Robert.

"I am sure you know, Mr. West, the early Jewish priesthood did not accept the divinity of Jesus. They could not comprehend how he could be the son of Yahweh, because Yahweh could not possibly procreate with an earth woman. There was no way, then, to understand the scientific achievements that would make such a thing possible without intercourse. The 'second coming' is a promise made by Jesus; it is a Christian concept, but as a professor of comparative religions, I can tell you that the promise is given something of a timeframe: it is said that anyone living during the creation of the State of Israel (when the Jews would return to their promised land - the Diaspora in reverse, if you will) will be alive to see the 'Second Coming,' which may be, now, understood as the return of the planet of the 'immortals.' Your book states, Ms. Brooks, that it is believed that this planet comes quite close to Jupiter. If it is nearing this position, I think it entirely likely that scouts would be sent to earth to determine the growth and development of our civilization. You have stated in your book that the Ark of the Covenant was a way to communicate biological information to this distant planet. With that capability lost for thousands of years, I think it likely another method was devised to investigate our progress."

"It seems to me, Rabbi, that you have been giving these matters a great deal of thought," remarked Penny.

"I have indeed, Ms. Brooks! I found your book most stimulating and your conclusions reasonable based on the World War II project and the reverse-engineering that you have done at your Foundation," he replied.

"Would you be willing to come to New York City to work with us on this project?" asked Penny. "We need to be very mindful of the faith that has sustained people for thousands of years. I have no desire to trample on religious objects of faith; I just want the truth to be presented in a manner that respects that faith. I think you could be of enormous help to that end. Will you come?" she asked.

"Where would I live, Ms. Brooks? I am an old man very set in my ways."

"There is an apartment available in the same building where the Foundation has its suite of offices and where Robert and I have our condo. You would have your privacy, but we would be readily available if you needed anything. The Foundation would lease this apartment for you and pay the consulting fee we discussed," she said.

"That is most generous and it would be wonderful to see my family, they all live in New York City," he responded. "I can be ready to leave in about three days; I can hardly wait to see the Ark and what it is capable of doing."

"We will make the flight arrangements and will be at the gate when you arrive. Is there anything else that we can do to assist you, Rabbi?" asked Penny.

"No, No. I have someone to care for my property here. It is just a matter of routine household chores and packing. Saying goodbye to friends, you know?"

"I understand. We will be on our way, Rabbi. We are delighted that you will be joining us," Penny said as she and Robert stood to leave.

The next three days were uneventful. Penny leased Minkowski's apartment and saw it furnished with anything the man might want and stocked the refrigerator with kosher foods. When they picked him up at JFK, he seemed much younger, perhaps like a teenager the first time out on his own. When he saw his apartment, he was astonished, "I am not used to such luxury, Ms. Brooks, but believe me, I shall try to endure," he said with a wide grin on his face.

The following day they were to meet with a bishop from the New York City diocese that included the famed St. Patrick's Cathedral. This would be, to be sure, the more difficult meeting to-date and probably would not be taking place at all if not for the help of Jonathan Mc Carthy, the very highly regarded New York City DA who was very active in church affairs. They had remained good friends even though he had been disappointed at Robert's decision to leave the prosecutor's office. After his wife died leaving him childless, he had become a surrogate grandfather to Penny's children and spent many Sundays with them for brunch and walking in Central Park. He had, also, been invited to go with them to Hunter Mountain for their next experiment with the Ark. He had set up the meeting with the bishop and was asked to join Penny and Robert at the meeting.

"Bishop, thank you for coming," began Penny, "I know that the Vatican See is not very happy with me, but I think it important that an organization that shepherds so many people be involved in this project. What we may do in the next few weeks and months could change a lot of peoples' belief systems - I do NOT think it should - which is why you should be involved. Rabbi Minkowski, who will be a part of our team said it better than I ever could, somewhat paraphrased: "I have always believed the day would come when I would be able to comprehend with my intelligence what my heart always knew." No longer do we have to choose between our hearts and our minds. Please help us build a bridge that will carry all your believers, safely, to the other side," Penny finished.

"I can see that you are sincere, Ms. Brooks. I am not authorized by the Vatican to become a part of your research group, but I would like to be a part of it to determine for myself the truths that you will be writing about. If I agree with your conclusions, I will see that the Christian flock is well represented," he said.

"That's a little enigmatic, but we will be glad to accept your participation on those terms. Welcome aboard, Sir," Penny replied as she and then Robert shook hands. "We will be conducting our next experiment, at midnight, the day after tomorrow. If you will be here, at the Foundation's office, by 10:00PM, we will ride together in a limousine. It was February and bitter cold. In addition to eight large thermoses of coffee, Penny decided she should take some sandwiches and some candy bars (and a bottle of whiskey for those who wanted to 'sweeten' their coffee). This was to be their longest session to-date. Robert had arranged for a generator and an electric heater for a small portable hut to be used in extreme weather conditions that added another SUV to their group of vehicles climbing Hunter Mountain.

The roads had been well plowed, although there was hard-packed snow on the road that was very shiny and slippery, but they made it to their site without incident.

The Ark was activated at exactly midnight and the two religious men stood absolutely still - in shock. The bishop crossed himself and Penny could hear a whispered, "Mary, Mother of God;" and the rabbi muttered some words in Hebrew. We saw the same light show as our previous experiments for the first hour, but then something new began to occur. Lights from many different parts of the sky seemed to join the orange globe until it grew in size to equal the size of the full moon. It was equally impressive and scary given its size. We watched as it grew larger and larger and then it just disappeared like a light bulb that has been turned off or a balloon that has burst! Penny heard a lot of "What the f---!!!" And then, "Sorry Father, sorry Rabbi."

On the ride home, the bishop spoke first, "that was the most impressive thing I have ever witnessed. Do you think that there is intelligent life operating those lights or ships or whatever they are?"

"Yes, Sir," responded Robert. "We have digital photographs that show that there is a disc at the center of each of those individual lights. "Something' is piloting those ships, but we do not believe that they are humanoid, but a creature especially created as part of the ship."

"Do you think it possible that someone besides Yahweh created those beings? Could it be an evil force that we are watching? What if this is Satan's hand at work?" he asked.

"Until we make some kind of intelligent contact, we can not know the answers to those questions, Father," replied Penny, "but it is clear that whoever is behind this phenomenon, they have been watching us for a long time, based on a historical analysis done by a member of our team. While the modern era began with World War II, there are many incidences of strange things in the sky throughout recorded history. I will give you a copy of that list when we reach the office; I think you will find it most impressive," she finished.

There was a car, with government plates, parked outside their building as they parked in front of the Foundation's office. Two men in dark suits opened their car doors as Penny, Robert and Jonathan Mc Carthy got out of their car and helped the bishop and rabbi out of the limousine. The government men walked toward them. "Ms. Brooks, I am Jeffrey Grove and this is Melvin Mathews; we are from the National Security Agency and we must speak privately with you and your husband." Penny looked at Robert who looked at McCarthy; he nodded his head slightly and the three turned to the two religious men and said their goodnights. It was nearly 3AM and the government was still awake; how odd, thought Penny as they made their way to the office with both men in tow.

"Please have a seat, gentlemen, and tell us what brings you here at 3AM," said Robert.

"The government has been receiving telephone calls from all over the country from frightened citizens who believe we are being invaded by creatures from outer space. We have been asked to insist that you cease and desist with your experiments with this laser that you have created. Telephone systems from the White House, the CIA, NASA and even the FBI are overloaded. This represents a threat to our national security. If you do not agree to comply with this order, we have been authorized to confiscate this device. Is that understood?" asked Grove.

Jonathan McCarthy spoke first. "Do you have a cease and desist order signed by a judge?"

"No, Sir, but we can have one within the hour if you feel it necessary," replied Grove.

"Let me have a look at your credentials," replied McCarthy. Both men opened their I.D. wallets and McCarthy nodded to Penny and Robert.

"Are you saying that we will never be able to conduct these experiments, again?" asked Penny.

"I cannot answer that question, Mrs. West, I suggest you contact Andrew Spade at the number on this card. He should be at his office by 8AM tomorrow, or rather, this morning," replied Grove. Both he and Mathews then turned and left the office.

"That sure puts a damper on things." Jonathan Mc Carthy was the first to speak.

"What are our legal rights, Jonathan, if they try to confiscate the Ark?" asked Penny.

"You have none when it comes to a matter of national security. If they perceive what you are doing as a threat, they can do whatever they deem necessary. There is nothing I, nor any attorney can do to prevent the confiscation." He was very pensive for a few moments and then said, "You have made friends with the prime minister of Israel; I suggest you contact him as soon as possible and get that device out of the country. Don't delay. Call him, now! It's not lunch time, yet, over there; I have to get to some sleep, I have to be in court in five hours," he finished. They all shook hands and Jonathan left.

"What do you think, Robert, is he right? Get the Ark out of the country?" Penny asked.

"It's that, Penny, or find a deserted Caribbean Island and I don't think we have time to look for one," he finished.

"I'd better put a call through, now. He may be out of the office," Penny spoke in a weary voice as she made her way to her office. She was surprised to be put right through to the prime minister and, when she finished explaining the situation, the prime minister surprised her further by offering the perfect solution.

"Ms. Brooks, why don't you open a branch office of your Foundation in Israel? The State of Israel will be happy to work with the Foundation to continue your experiments. In the meantime, I can make the arrangements for the Ark to be flown to Israel and housed in a safe place in Tel Aviv until we make a few decisions together. Does that sound acceptable?"

"It sounds like a perfect solution, Mr. Prime Minister, thank you. Can this be done quickly?" she asked.

"I will have agents at your door in about two hours. You may have to wake people at Columbia University to let you into the safe, but a plane will be waiting at JFK as soon as you can get there with the Ark. You and your husband would probably like to accompany the Ark. Bring the children, too; I will look forward to seeing all of you and will have my secretary make all the arrangements for your stay," he finished.

"Thank you, Mr. Prime Minister. We look forward to seeing you, again," she replied. Penny explained the conversation to Robert.

"He sure is efficient," said Robert. "What about the children, do you want to take them?" he asked.

"Yes, I'll get them ready. They can sleep on the plane. I am sure they both will enjoy the adventure of rushing off to the airport in the wee hours of the morning," she responded. "You'd better call Dave MacIntyre to open the safe at the university. He is going to be really disappointed to see the Ark leave."

After hot chocolate on the airplane the children went back to sleep. Penny was still amazed that within three hours of being told by the U.S. Government to stop their experiments, the Ark was on its way to Israel with the cooperation of the prime minister. She wondered how close they had really come to losing it to the government, never to see it operational again. Dave MacIntyre told Robert that he would resign his position at Columbia and accepted the full-time position with the Foundation that Robert had previously offered. He couldn't imagine doing any work, for the rest of his life, that was more important than the work he had been doing for the Foundation. His wife, who was Jewish, was delighted with the chance to live in Israel. It would be a month before he would be able to relinquish his position at Columbia, but he would be available to fly over for the next experiment in two weeks, if they kept to the planned timetable.

The *Renaissance Tel Aviv* was a delightful hotel right on the Mediterranean Sea and the children couldn't wait to get into their bathing suits. Fortunately, Nina, their nanny could take them wading while Robert and Penny accompanied the Ark to the University of Tel Aviv where it would be housed until, or if, they decided to make other arrangements. They were expected and taken to a sub-basement in one of the main buildings of the University where the Ark would be housed. The security arrangements were better than expected; the safe was equal to the one they'd had custom-made, but this one was said to withstand a direct hit by a nuclear bomb (preparations based on the precarious nature of life for everyone in Israel). The security guard went over all the arrangements and answered all of Robert's questions. He was satisfied; they thanked the guard and left with the knowledge that only Robert or Penny had access to the safe until further arrangements were made. They spent the afternoon on the beach with the children, but would spend the next day with a real estate agent who would show them office space to open their branch office of the Foundation.

Within three days they had found the perfect office space and furnished it. Dave MacIntyre would be the Director of Research at the Tel Aviv office and would hire his own staff as soon as he was available. One of the scientists who had been working with Dave would also move to Israel to continue his work.

When they returned to New York City they were in for another big surprise.; the government was waiting, again, at the entrance to their condo. It wasn't Jeffrey Grove and his cohort; it was the director of the CIA.

"Mr. and Mrs. West, do I understand your recent movements to mean that you have moved your laser to Israel?" he asked.

"I do not mean to be abrupt, Mr. Woodbridge, but is that really any of your business?" asked Robert. "We were told we could no longer operate the Ark in this country, we have made other arrangements! You people cannot have it both ways. You have no right to our business when you shut us down in this country!"

"You are right, Mr. West. I was against shutting you down, but the other agencies couldn't deal with the massive chaos from the citizenry. I have been kept informed by the director of NASA about your research. It is probably not news to you that the CIA has been monitoring this UFO phenomenon for years. We have a great interest in what you have learned about Adolf Hitler's project and what you have been able to do with the material you have found. It is quite astonishing, to tell you the truth. No one can know what I am about to tell you, but I think it is important for you to know, if you continue this work. May I come in to talk with you for a few minutes?" he asked.

"Yes, please come in," responded Robert, totally surprised by the man's demeanor and openness. As they all took a seat in the living room Robert offered the man a scotch, which he accepted and then he began where he had left off.

"Not even the president of the United States knows what I am about to tell you both; I am telling you because you both have demonstrated a serious interest in engaging whoever is behind this UFO phenomenon. Presidents come and go, sometimes as quickly as every four years, but this phenomenon has been with us for a very long time as has the interest of the CIA. We have not discerned any real threat from this phenomenon unless we try to take chase. We have, unfortunately, been able to shoot down some of the smaller ships and

have had some of the 'pilots,' for the lack of a better word, in captivity, but they have not survived for very long. These pilots seem to be a cross between an insect, because their bodies are so fragile, and a reptile, because their skin has that rubberish feel," he paused.

"Mr. Woodbridge, has there been any kind of communication with these creatures?" asked Penny.

"One of the exo-biologists working with our team of experts was able to make rudimentary, mentally telepathic communication. Simple things like 'thirst,' or 'fruit.' While these creatures have a highly developed brain, it seems devoted to actually operating the ship through thought and not to maintaining the physical body. What it requires to survive seems to be an unbroken link to the machine. When it is separated from the ship for any length of time, it expires. We learned this too late for the survival of the creatures we were studying," said Woodbridge.

"I just had an interesting thought," said Robert. "The vehicles have been described as two saucers inverted, but you might have a better comparison to something in biological life, if you think of it as a carapace, and the creature a turtle." Woodbridge looked at Robert pensively for a moment.

"Mr. West, that is exactly the conclusion reached by one of our exo-biologists. That someone has created an artificial life form that

mimics the life of a turtle - a space turtle with incredible capabilities. Turtles on earth are incredibly slow, but those in these ships are believed to travel at the speed of thought from a brain that is a melding of the creature and its ship," he finished. All were quiet for a moment. "Mr. and Mrs. West, would the Foundation be willing to work with the CIA on a super-secret project? We are now better informed than when we had these creatures in captivity; we would like to capture another to see what we can learn about their creator and their intentions."

Penny was upset, "We will NOT help you to capture any of these creatures, Mr. Woodbridge, but I think that Robert and I would be willing to share any communications that we might have in the future. Would you agree, Robert?" she asked.

"May I ask where the Ark is being housed?" asked the Director.

"Let's just say that the Ark of the Covenant has gone home, Mr. Woodbridge," responded Penny. She watched his face carefully and although he tried to hide it, it was there; he was crestfallen. Penny had little doubt in her mind that the director of the CIA had some hope of getting his hands on the laser.

Epilogue

The next few weeks were hectic, getting Dave MacIntyre settled in Tel Aviv at the Foundation's new office and acquiring the electronics he needed for his new lab. The experiments continued, on schedule, and proved to be more of what they had already encountered. They all began to wonder if they would ever have a close encounter that they had read about in the lore surrounding the UFO phenomenon or see any of the creatures that the CIA director talked about.

Dave had decided to try some messages, through telepathy, using advanced mathematics to see if he would get a response. He did. The inhabitants of those ships were no mere turtles; they were capable of solving complex mathematical problems that were communicated by a small laser that etched symbols in the ground. Dave began to grasp their language and soon began to realize that some of the phraseology reminded him of the 'crop circles' he had seen in a book showing those throughout fields in England. He understood that some of the mathematics were expressing the double helix of DNA, but not what was actually being said about the DNA. Were they analyzing the human structure? Is that what they were saying? That they were here as scientists?

It was three months later as they all stood watching another magnificent light show that Penny had a remarkable experience. There was no sound accompanying the experience just the phrase inside her head, "We mean no harm. Mean us no harm."

The whole group was astounded! Breakthrough! Contact! All the wonderful excitement that goes with discovery. A whole cacophony of questions were coming from the group for Penny to ask, but she wanted the answer to a more pressing question, "Do you come from another planet in our solar system, the planet of Yahweh and Jesus? From our creator?" An hour passed and the group began to think that maybe Penny had imagined the experience, when she finally heard a response, again through what could only be mental telepathy, "We come from the same house." Did 'house' mean the same as solar system or another planet? The group was convinced that *house* meant same solar system. Which planet and why were they here? Were they watching the nearing of this distant planet?

Penny thought back to this incredible journey that had begun four years ago with the attempt on the lives of her grandparents and the discovery of Hitler's secret project of World War II. Her grandparents did not live to see where that road would lead, but she was convinced, more than ever, that they were watching from another point of view - that they still existed in another state of life.

Penny was convinced that Artur Goldberg had it right all along; this distant planet would return to a position near the planet of Jupiter after a long journey and this was the real meaning of the 'Second Coming' and that all those alive on earth should expect visitors from the planet of our creator soon after the year 2012 A.D.

The promised 'Second Coming' has gone too long unfulfilled for many people to believe that it has any real relevance in the modern world, but perhaps they will find a renewal of their faith if they understand that the 'Second Coming' promise is predicated on the return of a planet to our solar system. A planet with an advanced society that has conquered death; a society of immortals. Will we be ready to accept the gift of immortality, offered once again by a stranger in our midst?

Penny was about to crawl into bed when Robert came to the bedroom door and spoke, "Prime Minister Eckstein is on the phone and wants to speak with us; please pick up the phone." He left to go back to the extension in the kitchen.

"Yes, Mr. Eckstein, what can we do for you?" Penny asked.

"We have had some severe weather in the northern part of our country and it appears that lightning struck one of the smaller spaceships. It crashed with three beings on board. They are alive. I think you should come as soon as possible," he finished.

AFTERWORD

Fact or Fiction?

1) Adolf Hitler, Ante Pavelic, Simon Wiesenthal and Billy Graham are real, public and historical personages.

2) Ante Pavelic *was* granted autonomy over Croatia during WWII.

3) A Franciscan Order *was* in charge of the Jasenovac concentration camp in Croatia during WWII.

4) Croatia is believed to have turned over its entire treasury to the Vatican at the end of WWII.

5) Hitler had a keen interest in finding and/or stealing religious objects of faith but, to my knowledge, he never found the Ark of the Covenant.

6) I believe the Ark of the Covenant is, in fact, the device that I have described in this book. My conclusion is based, in part, on the biblical reference to Uzza and other biblical descriptions of the strange properties of this device. You can read for yourself, in biblical literature, that upon touching the Ark Uzza became ill and his body was covered with oozing boils - a remarkably good description of radiation poisoning.

7) Also, check the reference about the 'stones or tablets' that Jewish legend states were sapphires and NOT the image we retain in our collective memory of Charlton Heston carrying two large, gray, stone tablets down from the mount. (JewishEncyclopedia.com)

8) The UFO phenomenon can no longer be denied; our government is at a loss as to how to explain or deal with it. Until there is some overt threat, the government will continue to deny something it cannot explain or control. It has been around since biblical days; you will read more about it in the next two books in this trilogy.

9) Others have hypothesized a 'missing planet' in our solar system, perhaps where the asteroid belt is positioned. In the next book in this trilogy, you will learn more about this missing planet and my own discovery of 1996, announced at the International Forum for New Science about the 'hidden message' of the Great Pyramid at Giza.

(over)

If you enjoyed this book, please watch for the next in this trilogy and send your comments to the author: bjatwell@yahoo.com

www.ingramcontent.com/pod-product-compliance
Lightning Source LLC
Chambersburg PA
CBHW020926310726
48980CB00005B/402

* 9 7 8 0 6 1 5 1 4 4 9 2 4 *